BOYD MATHESON

BOYD MATHESON

•

James Clay

AVALON BOOKS
NEW YORK

PRINTED IN THE UNITED STATES OF AMERICA
ON ACID-FREE PAPER
BY HADDON CRAFTSMEN, BLOOMSBURG, PENNSYLVANIA

For Lorilyn: a wonderful wife
and good editor.

Chapter One

Boyd Matheson's eyes opened and he looked about cautiously. The sky was slashed with red, as if a wound had opened up in the heavens. Surrounding him were the nervous sounds of morning: small varmints skittering about in search of food, birds making defiant noises as they flew from one perch to the next. The buzz of insects added to the cacophony of discordant sounds.

Matheson's instincts told him that danger was near. He closed his eyes, feigning sleep. He could hear nothing unusual. But inside him, he could feel an awful twitch. He wanted a smoke. Maybe he could hold off until after breakfast. Matheson forgot the instincts, folded back his blanket and got off the canvas that had served as a bed. He stretched, then began to build a fresh fire out of the embers where last night's dinner had been cooked.

The blaze began to spew warmth against the cool Arizona morning. Matheson had just hung a coffee pot over the fire when the coughing overtook him. This had long ago become a morning routine. Boyd stepped away from the fire, bent over and hacked loudly. Birds took off from a nearby tree, giving Matheson a bitter laugh that mingled with his cough.

When the spell ended, Matheson breathed deeply. He was beginning to feel relaxed when something hard slammed against the back of his skull. Red flashed across his eyes and Matheson dropped to the ground. Instinctively, he rolled and buoyed back onto his feet. A fist smashed against his jaw and Matheson again plunged to the ground. This time, boyish laughter cascaded over him.

"He sure don't look tough now, does he, Henry?" said the man who had just given Matheson a sore jaw.

"You're right 'bout that, Al."

"He'll look even worse hangin' from a tree," Al said. "Git up gunfighter, we got a long ride in front of us."

As Boyd's eyes focused, he saw two young men standing over him. Both had six-shooters pointed in his direction. He spoke in a casual voice as if discussing the weather. "Where would we be riding to?"

"Tucson," Al said. "You killed a rich man's son. Now that rich man is gonna give some of his cash to Henry and me for bringin' you back and hangin' you from a tree on his property. There'll be a picnic after they cut you down. 'Course, you probably won't be up to eatin' much."

The two boys exploded with garish laughter. Boyd assessed his captors as he got back onto his feet. They were both young, with hair the color of sand and wearing identical brown jackets—brothers, likely. Their faces were unshaven and their eyes slightly glazed. The young men weren't drunk but they had been drinking.

Matheson kept his voice calm, speaking in a monotone. "I'm up to eating good right now. How about some breakfast before we get started?"

Henry looked edgy and confused. He glanced toward Al, who seemed to be the leader of the two. "Happy to accept your hospitality, gunfighter," Al said hesitantly.

The three men walked back to the fire. Al and Henry stood on one side with their guns pointed at Matheson while he prepared coffee and bacon from the other side. Matheson's saddle pillowed his bedroll. He was careful not to glance at the blanket on that bedroll as he retrieved items from the two large saddle bags.

"Guess it wouldn't interest you gents any if I told you I killed that rich man's son in self defense." Matheson spoke as he poured coffee into three cups.

Al tensed up. He was expecting Matheson to throw the coffee at him. When the gunfighter handed two cups across the flames in a careful, courteous manner,

Al began to laugh. "That don't mean a pitcher of warm spit to me."

Each brother took one cup, then Al continued. "Yeah. I saw the fight. He drew on you first. But my brother and me is businessmen, right Henry?"

Henry nodded his head and pushed out a laugh. Al kept talking. "Last week we killed us a man who didn't cotton to us takin' horses off his ranch."

Boyd listened to his captors brag as he placed three strips of bacon over the fire. The brothers were killers, but they were also fools. So far, they hadn't asked Matheson about his guns. He wasn't carrying any weapon and that appeared to satisfy them. Alcohol must have blurred their judgment. Boyd hoped the coffee would help that along. It might be true that java could sober a man up in the long run, but the gunfighter had seen coffee give a touch of giddiness to many a drunk before it worked its cure.

A sizzling sound accompanied by smoke came from the meat. "Be a spell before the bacon's ready," Boyd said. "Why don't we sit and be comfortable." Matheson squatted down in front of the bedroll and drank from his mug. The brothers sat across from him.

Al shot a cruel smile over the flames. "Care for a smoke, gunfighter?" He set his cup on the ground and pulled a tobacco pouch and papers from a pocket in his jacket.

They knew. After the gunfight in Tucson, Boyd Matheson had rolled himself a cigarette without really thinking about it. One puff had sent him into a violent coughing fit. He had almost fallen over. And Al had witnessed it all.

Boyd spoke in a jittery voice, "No thanks."

The brothers laughed. Henry rolled two cigarettes as his brother kept a gun pointed at Matheson. As they lit the smokes in slow elaborate gestures, Al continued to taunt his prisoner. "Come on. Have a smoke. Goes real good with coffee."

Matheson had been biting his lips. He nodded nervously. "Yes, yes. Obliged."

Al placed a paper in the tobacco pouch and sent it flying through the smoke. Matheson caught it in midair. His fingers trembling noticeably as he began to roll a cigarette. While the brothers laughed at him, Matheson thought about his sore jaw. Al had hit him with his right hand. His gun hand. That hand would be getting numb by now.

The brothers watched expectantly as Boyd Matheson lit his cigarette and inhaled deeply. A peaceful look came over his face, then Matheson suddenly bent over into an uncontrolled cough. He collapsed backwards onto his bedroll. The brothers' laughter now became hysterical. Matheson pulled his Colt .45 from under the blanket and pumped two bullets into Henry. As the young man's laughter turned into a horrible high pitched scream, his brother jumped up and fired at Matheson. But Al's numb hand made for a bad shot and he missed Matheson, who had lurched into a fast roll. One shot was all Al got. He dropped his gun and stumbled backwards as a bullet from Matheson's Colt ripped into his chest. Al was dead before he hit the ground.

Boyd Matheson rose slowly. The birds and critters in the woods were now still. The only sound was popping grease coming from the fire. Matheson stared at the two bodies on the other side of the flames. Both were lying at a comfortable distance from their guns.

Colt in hand, Matheson first checked Al, then moved to Henry. The young man was still breathing but his eyes had a distant, glassy look that Matheson had seen too often.

"He lied, you know," Henry said. "That brother of mine killed the rancher by hisself. I helped steal the horses. I shoulda never listened to Al."

Matheson nodded his head.

"There's a girl back in Tucson," Henry said.

"You want me to write her?" Matheson asked. It surprised him but for some reason he really wanted to help the dying young man.

Henry smiled at Boyd Matheson, as if they had been close friends for years. "You can't. I don't know the girl's name. We'd never spoke. But we'd sorta looked at each other—you know."

"Yes, I know."

"I wanted to speak with her. Maybe coulda made a new life . . . away from my brother . . . California maybe. I wanted to speak . . ."

Henry talked a little more but Matheson could no longer understand the words. He found himself guessing at Henry's age. Seventeen or so, probably. Al was maybe a year or two older.

After Henry died, Boyd returned to the fire and ate some of the bacon. It was a strange but necessary act. He couldn't waste too much food. There was a long day ahead and two corpses that had to be buried.

When he had finished eating, Matheson spotted the tobacco pouch lying on the ground. He angrily picked it up and hurled it into the flames. He realized how lucky he had been. What if that cigarette had really pushed him into a coughing fit? It could have. Those fits were coming on more and more frequently, and especially when he tried to have a smoke.

Matheson vowed that he'd toss away his own tobacco that morning. But there were two bodies to bury first. As he went about his work, the gunfighter mused on the many changes in his life. Changes that went far beyond the coughing and occasional shortages of breath that now plagued him.

He had never enjoyed killing, but now he found himself worrying over details that hadn't bothered him before. For one, he was starting to care about the age of his victims. Matheson was thirty-four. Henry and Al had looked almost like children to him. Staring at them over the fire, he wished he could shoot only to wound. But both men had guns pointed at him, making that notion impossible. In Tucson, it had grieved him that the rich man's son he had killed left behind a wife and child.

James Clay

Matheson looked down at the two fresh graves. It seemed wrong not to say words, yet he didn't know which words to say. Maybe he should carry a Bible in one of his saddle bags.

Matheson angrily stalked away from the graves. Those were the kind of thoughts a gunfighter couldn't afford to have. He quickly doused the fire, packed up his gear and saddled his horse. He had mounted when he remembered his vow to toss away his own tobacco and papers. He bit his lower lip, cursed himself, then rode off with the tobacco still close at hand.

Chapter Two

It was getting close to midday when Boyd Matheson rode into the town of Gradyville. He paid only scant attention to his surroundings. He wouldn't be in town long.

A ghost suddenly ran in front of him, startling the gunfighter. She was a beautiful young woman with blond hair and a slightly tomboyish face that was now contorted by fright. Matheson halted his horse. The woman didn't seem to notice him. She dashed onto the boardwalk and into a general store. A small brown dog frantically scrambled behind her.

Boyd closed his eyes. The girl only looked like Ann, he told himself.

The dog's wild yapping could be heard from inside the store. A shot was fired in response. The barking stopped and a woman screamed, shattering the trance

9

Matheson seemed to be in. He quickly looked around him. There were several people on both sides of the street. They were all glancing furtively at the store, while pretending that nothing unusual was happening.

"Stop it! He's an old man! You'll kill him!" The woman's voice was filled with hopeless despair as if she knew her words wouldn't be heeded.

Matheson jumped down and flipped his horse's reins around a hitching rail as he moved quickly into Remick's General Store. Two men were pouring a barrel of flour over an old man who was sprawled in front of a long counter. A third man held the blond haired woman.

"Yessir, all sortsa accidents happen to a man who don't pay his rent," one of the men said as he shook the last particles of flour from the barrel and tossed it through the store window.

The young woman yelled something, then broke loose from her captor and ran toward the man who had thrown the barrel. He rammed a fist into her right shoulder, spinning the girl and knocking her to the floor. The man who had been holding her, embarrassed that she had escaped, grabbed her arms and forced her to her feet in a rough manner, pinning an arm behind her back.

Boyd Matheson had watched this scene as he entered the door. No one had noticed him. Boyd pegged the man who threw the barrel as the leader of the group, since the jasper who held the girl kept looking at him. The one who had helped pour out the flour was more difficult to peg. He was younger than his two companions—in his very early twenties. He appeared edgy and uncertain. When the girl fell he had instinctively held out his arm for a moment, like he was trying to catch her.

The area in front of the counter was now covered by a white mound shaped something like a coffin. Matheson purposely made slow heavy steps toward the group. "You gents have just made a heap of trouble for yourselves."

"Whaddya mean?" asked the barrel-thrower.

"You're going to have to pay for a new window, the flour, and if need be, a doctor."

The three men who had been wrecking the store laughed nervously. The man who was holding the girl spit in Matheson's direction. "Stranger, you got some real fool notions."

A desire to tear the spitter apart welled up inside Boyd Matheson. But he kept control, realizing the act was an attempt to distract him from the leader, who was advancing on him quickly. Matheson whirled and feigned a punch at his adversary's head. The man moved both of his arms up. With rapid speed, Matheson delivered a series of hard punches to the gut. The leader bent over and Matheson pushed him into the younger man, who was advancing to help his comrade. Both men tumbled onto the floor, sending up a white cloud of flour.

The younger man rolled to his feet, his face scorched with humiliation. He began to charge at

Matheson but slipped on the white powder and stumbled into a hard right fist that Matheson landed on his nose. He flopped back onto the floor.

"Watch out!" The woman screamed in warning.

Boyd spun around and saw the spitter standing only a few feet away with his gun drawn.

"Don't move!" the gunman shouted.

The girl had been pushed against the counter. The leader was now standing in a slightly bent position, gingerly holding his ribcage. To Matheson's surprise the younger man was still lying on the floor.

"Good work, Pete." The leader's words whistled out.

Pete smiled broadly. He was proud of himself and, with the leader injured, was trying to take control of the situation. "Think I'll teach this jasper a lesson about mindin' his own business."

Pete moved swiftly toward Matheson. He didn't notice the white mound beside him stirring. A figure suddenly rolled out of the flour and plowed against Pete's legs. As Pete stumbled at him, Matheson grabbed his right arm and twisted it till the gun fell to the floor. He pushed Pete toward the leader and drew his Colt.

"Throw it down!" Matheson shouted. The leader obeyed, tossing his half drawn six-shooter into a small hill of flour. The man's face was almost the color of the white powder. He seemed to be having problems breathing.

The old man placed one hand on the blond woman's shoulder as he gradually stood up. "Don't worry. It'll take more than trash like those three to stop me."

Matheson carefully watched the young man who was also getting back onto his feet. The kid untied his bandana and held it over his nose, which was bleeding. Without speaking, he obeyed Boyd's instructions and tossed his gun to the floor.

The kid's behavior seemed very strange to Matheson. But he figured he could worry about it later.

"Put all of your money on the counter. Right now."

Pete winced. "You gotta—"

"Now!" Matheson shouted. The three men did what they were told.

Boyd turned to the young woman. "Ma'am, would you mind counting the money to make sure there's enough to cover all the damage these gents caused?"

The young woman quickly complied. "This money will almost pay for a new window."

"They owe you more than that." Matheson gave the threesome a sarcastic grin. "You can vamoose now, gents, but leave your hoglegs where they are. I reckon they'll fetch a good price."

"You can't do that!" Pete shouted. He was shifting his weight from one foot to the other rapidly.

Matheson smiled and spoke in a quiet but firm voice. "Yes I can."

Pete glanced at his two companions. They remained silent. Pete glared angrily at Matheson. "Stranger, you're diggin' your own grave. This ain't the finish of it."

The three gunmen stomped out of the store wearing empty holsters. After they were gone, the young woman spoke haltingly to the newcomer. "Thank you sir, we're—"

"The name is Boyd Matheson." The gunman awkwardly nodded his head, holstered his gun and took off his hat.

The young woman nodded her head. "Mr. Matheson. I'm Laurel Remick. This is my grandfather, Cassius."

Cassius Remick was a short, stocky man with a thick head of what Matheson supposed was gray hair. Like the rest of him, Cassius' head was covered by flour.

"Pleased to meet you, Mr. Matheson." The old man took a step toward Boyd with his hand extended. He suddenly noticed the congealed flour on his palms, stopped and looked himself over. "Them owlhoots turned me into a spook. Or tried to. I ain't dead yet."

Laurel's face clouded with emotion as she looked at her grandfather. Without speaking, she grabbed a towel off a nearby shelf and began to brush the old man's face and hands. "Oh, Grandfather—" she started, but stopped as her voice broke.

Her expression changed as a pattering sound came from behind the counter. The small brown mutt that had followed the girl into the store now darted around the counter. "Perkins!" Laurel bent down and embraced the small furry creature as if it were a child. She cradled the animal in her arms as she stood up. "I was so afraid—" Again, the young woman stopped speaking but this time her voice was broken by laughter as Perkins licked her face.

Cassius Remick looked at Matheson. "That fool dog gets more attention from my granddaughter than I do!" He tried to sound angry, but couldn't bring it off.

"That's not true, Grandfather." The girl spotted the humor in the old man's eyes and they laughed together, more with relief than merriment. Then the young woman and old man seemed to fall into an exhausted state of silence. Even Perkins was quiet.

Breaking a silence was not one of Matheson's skills, but he tried anyway. "I'm a man with some time on my hands. If you folks would be kind enough to allow me, I'd enjoy helping you put things back in order."

"You've done so much for us already, Mr. Matheson," Laurel said as she gently placed the dog on the floor and shooed him away from stepping in the flour. "We can't let you do a thing more."

"Sure we can!" Cassius Remick shouted. "If the man wants to pass some time hammerin' boards across a busted window, I ain't givin' him no argument."

Boyd followed the old man into a back room of the store where they located enough wood to cover the window. He threw two quick glances at Laurel. He stopped on the second try when his eyes fused briefly with hers.

Laurel Remick did look a lot like Ann, Matheson thought. And she was probably a year or so short of twenty. Ann had been nineteen when Boyd met her.

Laurel began to sweep up the flour as Cassius and Boyd boarded up the window. Perkins slowed down both projects by running through the flour, then jumping on Laurel and the old man. Matheson pegged the mutt as being completely worthless.

Boyd was about to hammer a nail into a plank that he and Cassius had placed across the window when a weight suddenly pulled at his midriff. Perkins swayed on Matheson's gun belt, then dropped to the floor leaving a trail of flour on Matheson's pants. The small dog barked playfully, then ran toward his mistress.

"Perkins likes you, Mr. Matheson," Laurel's eyes beamed at the gunfighter. "You should feel honored."

Matheson smiled at the mutt who was now attacking the broom, then lifted his eyes to Laurel. "A man in my position can't be too fussy," Boyd tried to sound cordial. It surprised him that talking to the young woman made him nervous. "I've been in town for less than an hour and I've already made some enemies. Guess I'll take whatever friends I can find."

Laurel's voice turned serious. "It reflects well on a man when he has the kind of enemies you do, Mr. Matheson." She paused then continued. "If you stay, I believe you'll find it easy to make friends."

An awkward silence followed—awkward, but short. Perkins knocked the broom out of Laurel's hand, grabbed some of the straws in his mouth and began to run around the store. Laurel ran after him, grabbed the handle of the broom and began to shake it loose from the dog's clenched teeth.

All of this was accompanied by good-natured laughter. Boyd reckoned that Perkins had brought a lot of joy into the lives of two folks who badly needed it. Maybe the mutt wasn't so worthless after all.

Cassius Remick seemed to read Matheson's thoughts. He spoke in a quiet voice as they both bent down to lift another wooden plank. "My granddaughter found that mongrel about a year or so ago, when it weren't no more than a starvin' pup. Fool dog's been a blessin', I'll say that. Makes the girl smile. And there ain't been much to smile about 'round' here lately."

Matheson waited until the window was boarded up and Laurel was outside sweeping the glass from the boardwalk before he picked up on the old man's statement. "Why were those owlhoots giving you so much trouble?"

"In two words, Bull Grady."

"Is he the man the town is named for?"

"Yeah," the old man replied. "Named it that way hisself. Oh, Grady's done some good in his time. I ain't claimin' different. Came here in sixty-seven, folks say. Started a ranch and prospered by sellin' horses to the army; 'fore ya know it, Grady has a mine opened up and other folks start movin' in. Grady builds a few saloons, a hotel and a few other places and names the town after hisself. So far, nothin' wrong with that."

The door opened and Laurel returned with Perkins following behind her. Cassius continued. "But after awhile, Grady starts gettin' some real crazy notions. He reckons since he was here first and named the town, ever' one else is stayin' on his property and oughtta pay him for it. I built this here store myself and I ain't about to pay Bull Grady no rent!"

"Bull Grady reminds me of King Saul in the Bible," Laurel said. "He's got to have everything his way. He controls this whole town. Only some of us are trying to stand up to him. We have the sheriff, George Stuart, on our side. I ran to fetch him when the trouble started, but he's out of town for a few hours."

"Reckon those men knew that when they came to collect for Bull Grady," Cassius said.

"They're cowards!" Laurel said with sudden intensity. She smoothed the front of her dress, paused, then spoke in a softer voice. "We would be honored if you would have dinner with us tonight, Mr. Matheson. I can't promise you anything special, but grandfather finds my cooking to be to his liking. And Cassius Remick is not an easy man to please."

Matheson looked at the floor to hide his embarrassment. He wanted very much to accept the invitation but knew he couldn't. "Thank you Miss Remick, a home cooked meal would taste mighty good, but I've got business matters that need taking care of. It's been a pleasure meeting you good folks . . ." Matheson stopped speaking, then continued. "I hope we meet again some time."

Boyd walked quickly out of the store. He couldn't

tell them about the business that had brought him to Gradyville, about the appointment he had that night with the man who had summoned him to the town. A man named Bull Grady.

Chapter Three

The desk clerk glanced at the name on the register and gave Matheson a nervous look. That didn't surprise the gunfighter. Cassius Remick had already told him that Bull Grady owned the hotel.

"I'll be wanting to take a bath," Matheson said.

"A tub will be brought right up, sir!" The clerk responded with an ingratiating smile.

Matheson's room was on the second floor of the three story building. The door had a lock, but the gunfighter instinctively propped a chair under the doorknob before starting to bathe. After the bath, Boyd put on some fresh clothes he had purchased in Tucson. After the tub was taken away, Matheson began to feel restless. The wire he had received in Tucson told him to remain in his hotel room until he was contacted. Easy enough instructions to follow, but . . .

Boyd Matheson wanted a smoke. He cursed himself for the horrible craving that coursed through his body, making him want to scream like a calf thirsting for milk. What was wrong with him anyhow? He had faced down many enemies in his life. Why couldn't he throw away a pouch of tobacco?

There was a loud knock at the door. Matheson took a deep breath then opened the door in a nonchalant manner. Facing him was the young man he had punched in the nose only a few hours ago.

"Is today your birthday?" Matheson asked.

The young man wasn't expecting the question. "What?" he replied.

"Notice you're wearing a brand new hogleg," Matheson nodded toward the six-shooter in his visitor's holster. "Wondered if it was a birthday present."

"Listen, Matheson—"

"You seem to know my name, don't be shy about telling me yours."

"Clay Adams."

"State your business, Adams."

"Mr. Grady wants to see you. Now."

Leaving the door open, Boyd walked over to the bedpost, lifted off his hat, then rejoined Adams. "I'm ready."

As they stepped into the hallway Matheson slammed the door fiercely, creating a loud bang. That surprised Clay Adams. It surprised Matheson too, but he gave no indication of it.

Boyd Matheson had been in this situation many

times before. People who wanted to hire gunfighters always went through a process of some kind to either hide their identity or let the hired gun know that they were above him. Matheson smiled inwardly. The folks who paid a gunfighter always wanted to feel above the man they needed to solve their problems.

Matheson usually remained quiet in these situations. But the gunfighter's way of doing things had been changing lately. As they left the hotel and squinted their eyes against the low hanging sun, Matheson spoke in a mocking voice to his companion. "I notice you changed your duds. I guess it'll take a while to brush all the flour off the clothes you were wearing before."

"Why don't you just shut up, Matheson?" Clay Adams snorted like an angry horse, then continued. "I got a job to do. Take you to Mr. Grady. After that, I hope I never see you again."

"You had a job to do this afternoon," Matheson replied. "As I recall, you spent most of the time lying down on the job. You must have been taking a rest. That punch on the nose didn't knock you out."

"I wasn't scared to fight you, Matheson!" Clay's voice was almost a shout.

"I know," Boyd replied.

Clay Adams was walking about a half step ahead of the gunfighter. He turned around and sputtered out a few words, unable to form a complete thought.

"You should have been afraid of me, but you

weren't," Matheson said. "So, why didn't you get up and do what Bull Grady had told you to do."

Clay's sputtering continued. "Well, uh, . . ."

"Maybe you didn't like the job much," Matheson interrupted. "Can't say I blame you. Pushing around an old man and his granddaughter. Not the kind of job I'd care for."

Clay Adams looked straight ahead, refusing to glance at his companion. The two men were walking toward the Fighting Bull Saloon. No surprise, Matheson thought. Bull Grady probably had an office in one of his saloons.

Directly across from the Fighting Bull, a large wagon was parked in front of the boardwalk. Two men were on the wagon. They seemed to be selling something to a small gathering of people. Matheson noted that business was being conducted very hastily. No one wanted to dither around that wagon.

Clay Adams angrily mumbled something that Matheson couldn't make out. Adams began trotting toward the wagon with the gunman directly behind him. The crowd dispersed immediately, leaving the businessmen on the wagon without any customers. Matheson noted that the two gents looked almost identical except that one was wearing a derby.

"Abner, get that rotgut of yours over to the Roman Holiday Saloon," Adams shouted as they neared the wagon. "You're getting yourself in big trouble."

"Now, don't go gittin' in a sweat, Mr. Adams," said

the man with the derby. "Some folks was just in a bit of a hurry for a jug; we was only bein' obligin'."

Abner turned toward Matheson and tipped his derby. "My name is Abner Tibbs." He nodded, returned his derby to his head, then pointed to the man beside him on the wagon. "This here is Dencel Tibbs. We're brothers."

As Matheson returned the greeting he took a close look at the Tibbs'. They were older men than the two brothers he had encountered that morning. Both were tall and muscular, but a hard life made worse by hard whisky was taking its toll. Their eyes oozed with the desperation and violence of men whose lives had been reduced to basic survival.

"My brother and me like to be good Samaritans," Abner said. "Be sure and let us know—"

"You two are working for Bull Grady and nobody else!" Adams' voice held more frustration than anger. "Now get that—"

"But Mr. Adams," Abner protested, "the sheriff said it would make no never mind if now and ag'in we sold some jugs—"

"Bull Grady is the law in this town!" Adams shouted. "I won't tell him about this if you get that tanglefoot where it belongs. And don't try selling it no more except to the Roman Holiday Saloon. Now move!"

Abner replied with a string of assurances that there would be no repetition of today's grievous misunderstanding, then he and his brother drove the wagon toward the Roman Holiday Saloon. Matheson chortled quietly to himself. He reckoned the Fighting Bull was Gradyville's most prominent saloon, while The Roman Holiday catered to the riff-raff.

Adams and Matheson resumed their walk. "It's good that Bull Grady has messengers like you," Matheson said. "Otherwise some folks might get the crazy notion that the sheriff is the law in this town."

"You're a good one to talk!" Adams turned and glared intensely at Matheson. Boyd was surprised by the depth of rage in the young man's eyes. "You're nothing but a hired gun. You'll do whatever Bull Grady tells you to do!"

"I'll listen to what Grady has to say." Matheson's voice carried a defiant undertone. "But I won't hop around the room just because he yells jump."

The two men entered the Fighting Bull, which was bustling with customers. No one seemed to take much notice as the two newcomers stepped through the swinging doors and headed up a stairway pressed against the left wall of the saloon. Matheson noted the barroom was ornately decorated, with thick purple curtains covering a window in the back, to the right of the bar. Matheson credited it to fear of Bull Grady that no drunken jasper had ever put a match to those fancy curtains.

Despite himself, Matheson was impressed by the elegant railing that ran along the stairs and across the second floor. Folks could stand at the railing and look down on the first floor. "Just like those saloons in Denver," the gunfighter whispered.

When they got up to the second level, they turned and headed along a balcony that connected three hallways. The first two had several rooms. The gunfighter shook his head slightly. It didn't take much thought to figure out what kind of business was conducted in those rooms. Matheson had been in many towns large and small and knew that some things were always pretty much the same.

But the third hallway was different. It was shorter and there was only one door which was located at the very end. The occupant of that lone room obviously wanted to remain apart from the business that surrounded him.

Clay Adams rapped twice on the door. A low rumbling came from inside. Adams opened the door and entered, nodding for Matheson to follow. "Here he is, Mr. Grady." Adams closed the door.

Adams and Matheson stood facing a large desk. Behind it the room's only window was blocked by another set of thick curtains, only these curtains were a deep black. A kerosene lamp was perched on the desktop, casting a yellow glow that penetrated only a fraction of the darkness that enveloped the room. A creaking sound began to fill the room as Matheson watched a huge shadow, seated behind the desk, turn and face the two new arrivals.

"You stupid fool!" The voice was guttural and

angry. "I told you to bring him up the back way. Now every barfly in town will know that I had a meeting with this gunfighter."

"I'm sorry Mr. Grady, but you said nothing about the back way. You must have forgot—"

The bulky figure lurched with surprising speed from the chair, stampeded around the desk and moved toward Clay Adams. Grady backhanded the young man across his face. It was a hard blow and Matheson was impressed that Adams managed to stand firm against it.

Bull Grady wasn't impressed. If anything the young man's stoic resistance inflamed Grady's anger. "Don't you ever speak like that to me!" the large man thundered, then he pointed a finger at Adams. "Remember this, little boy. All you've got is a broken down old farm run by your broken down mother who's getting too weak to scratch dirt. You lose your job with me and you've got nothing. Nothing!"

Clay's eyes closed half way with resignation and defeat. "I'm sorry, sir."

"Get the other lights on." Grady turned to the gunfighter. "Sit down, Matheson."

Without speaking Matheson sat on the one chair that stood in front of Grady's desk. He watched as Clay Adams ignited two lamps fastened to the side walls, then took his place behind the boss man.

Bull Grady was a massive man of about sixty. His thinning black hair was generously streaked with gray. Layers of flesh lay under his chin. The man would have looked harmless except for a fierce anger that burned in his eyes. That anger seemed to be what propelled and motivated him, making the rest of his body a lot of heavy, useless luggage.

Bull Grady sat down slowly in his large chair. Matheson reckoned that sitting down had to be a cautious undertaking for a man of Grady's weight. Bull glanced at his two companions and made a thin smile that looked like a small cut in the flesh of his face. Both men were where he wanted them to be. His universe was in order.

Grady took a cigar from a box on his desk and fired it up. He didn't offer a smoke to the hired help. "You know the sheriff, George Stuart?" he asked Matheson.

"I know about him."

"Kill him. As soon as Stuart is dead, Sonny here will give you your pay. One thousand dollars. Then you leave town and don't come back."

Clay Adams' eyes widened in shock. That kid is going to have to learn to control his emotions better if he hopes to get much older, Matheson thought. To Grady he said, "I need to know more."

"Why?"

"A man has to be cautious," Matheson replied in a calm monotone. "One thousand dollars is a lot of money. You could get someone to do it cheaper. One of your own boys, maybe."

Grady nodded his head, acknowledging that what Matheson had just said was true. "It's important to get this done just right." He paused and inhaled on his cigar. The room was beginning to fill up with cigar smoke. Boyd could feel a tightening in his chest.

"The problems started about four years ago," Grady explained. "A group of town idiots started a city council. I had my own man, Clarence Potts, elected mayor. I thought he'd keep the idiots in line, but Potts turned out to be a weakling. The members of the council began to refuse to pay rent for operating on my land. They even hired a sheriff. I tried to be reasonable with George Stuart, but he thinks that a piece of tin makes a man important. He's about to find out different."

Matheson was beginning to feel faint. He was trying not to breath the cigar smoke, but that was almost impossible. Two conflicting urges were pulling at him. He wanted to run from the smoke, but at the same time he had an urgent desire to light up a smoke himself.

Bull Grady didn't notice the gunfighter's discomfort. He continued speaking. "Clarence Potts is up for reelection. I want the weakling to stay in. I can provide a backbone. The council is running a pulpit pounder against him. Sheriff Stuart has been yapping a lot about how the balloting will be carefully watched. Says he wants to make sure that some citizens don't get too civic minded and vote more than once. A real funny man, George Stuart. But I'll have the last laugh and it will be at his funeral."

Perspiration was beginning to run down Matheson's

face. Breathing was becoming difficult. He had to cough before he could speak. "You still haven't answered my question. Why hire me?"

"You have a reputation," Grady answered. "When he learns you're in town, Stuart will look you up. You'll provoke him into a gunfight. After the sheriff's dead, you'll vamoose. All neat and tidy. Nothing to bring the rangers here."

With the mention of the rangers, everything began to make sense. The Arizona Rangers had been known to take over towns that men like Bull Grady were treating as a private fiefdom. They would provide the law until fair elections were held. But Arizona was a large territory with plenty to keep the rangers busy. The sheriff being killed by a transient gunfighter would not cause them to move into Gradyville.

"I'd become a fugitive," Matheson said. "Hunted by the rangers and every other lawman."

Bull Grady shrugged his shoulders. "You're getting well paid. You could disappear into Mexico."

"Sorry Mr. Grady, this may sound strange, but I don't break the law. I've killed, but only when it was necessary. George Stuart sounds like a fine man. I recommend you try to make peace with him." Matheson stood up and started toward the door. "The advice is free. Good-bye."

"Get back here, Matheson!" Grady roared, but the gunfighter didn't really hear him. He got outside of the office as quickly as possible, leaned against a side wall and began to gasp for air. After a few moments the pain in his chest began to subside. He looked up and saw a large cloud of smoke that hovered over the main floor of the Fighting Bull Saloon. He took a deep breath and walked toward the stairwell, keeping a steely expression. Some people in Tucson had seen him almost crumble from a coughing fit. That couldn't happen again. He walked steadily down the stairs, then held his breath while taking long fast strides out of the saloon.

Clay's eyes were once again wide with shock. He watched as Bull Grady laughed at the office door which Matheson had just slammed. The big man continued to chuckle as he sat down slowly. Clay Adams had never seen his boss act so happy. But Bull Grady's laughter was not infectious. It was frightening.

"The first plan didn't work," Grady waved his cigar. "So, we use plan two." He looked at Clay Adams. "It'll cost more blood but save me one thousand dollars. That's a better plan, don't you think?"

Chapter Four

Boyd Matheson ate dinner in the hotel dining room. He didn't linger over his food. Two drummers sitting at a table near him were smoking cigars, igniting that wretched twitch inside the gunfighter. Matheson left the hotel and walked swiftly down the boardwalk. He wasn't headed in any particular direction. He was silently cursing himself for being so weak.

Why couldn't he give up tobacco? The stuff was making him sick. He was sure of that. And it wasn't the kind of sick he had felt when he first started smoking at the age of eleven. His first cigarette had made him dizzy and, according to his ma, had turned his complexion green. This was more serious. The tobacco could be killing him.

Boyd brushed that thought from his mind. He tried to concentrate on tomorrow. Where would his next destination be? Maybe he should head for Tombstone. There was always plenty of work there for a man with his skills.

Matheson suddenly stopped. Across the road was Remick's General Store. With a feigned casualness, the gunfighter ambled half way across the road and eyed the lit window on the right side of the store. Laurel Remick's shadow moved gracefully across the white curtains. She appeared to be gathering up dishes from the evening meal.

Boyd realized that he could easily have been in that room with Laurel. He wished he had accepted her dinner invitation. A dog's playful yapping could be heard from inside the building. Matheson smiled to himself. Perkins was up to some new shenanigans.

The gunfighter approached the store, thinking that maybe he'd stop by for just a moment, see if there was anything more that he could do to help. Abruptly, he turned and walked back toward the saloon.

What possible good could he be to Laurel and her grandfather? He was leaving Gradyville at sunrise. He had already done what little good he could by refusing to kill the town's sheriff.

Matheson stopped and quickly rolled a cigarette. He knew sleep would never come if he didn't have an evening smoke.

He inhaled on the cigarette and continued to walk toward the Fighting Bull. Maybe there was one more thing to take care of before leaving Gradyville. He'd stop by the sheriff's office and tell him about Bull

Grady's offer. It went against everything a man in Matheson's situation was supposed to do, but the gunfighter didn't care. He'd warn the sheriff.

With a cigarette dangling from the side of his mouth, Boyd entered the saloon and headed directly for the bar. He settled in at the far left end of the bar, near an open window that diluted the clouds of smoke in the saloon. The barkeep quickly poured Matheson the whiskey he ordered, then returned to a conversation he was having with a group of regular customers at the opposite end of the bar. Matheson drank and smoked at a leisurely pace, enjoying his apparent anonymity.

It didn't last. From a mirror behind the bar, Boyd watched a short beefy man enter the Fighting Bull and walk directly toward him. "You Boyd Matheson?" The man asked.

"Yeah."

"The sheriff wants to talk to ya."

"What about?"

"Don't know. But ya better look 'im up. He's in his office. Know where that is?"

"I know," Matheson replied. He remembered seeing the sheriff's office when he had first ridden into town. Having delivered his message, the short man wandered off to jaw with the other patrons. Boyd noticed the man was obviously well acquainted with many of the customers and saloon girls. He was no stranger to the town. Boyd also noted that eyes were starting to flick in his direction, then turn away. The gunfighter paid them no heed. He slowly finished his whiskey and smoke, then strolled out of the saloon.

This was not a new experience for Matheson. Bull Grady had been right about one thing. Boyd Matheson had a reputation, and when he arrived in a town the local law usually took an interest. Boyd accepted that. Besides, this visit would give him a chance to fulfill his silent vow to inform the sheriff about Bull Grady's plans.

The sheriff's office was a squat two-story structure located between a gun shop and a hardware store. The office was dark, but a light shone from a second story window. Matheson reckoned the sheriff lived upstairs. As if confirming his notion, Matheson could hear a side door opening.

A tall lanky man stepped onto the second story porch of a stairway that ran up the right side of the building. "Would you be Sheriff Stuart?" Boyd called out the question as he looked up from the ground level.

"That's me," the sheriff replied casually as he closed the door behind him.

"I'm Boyd Matheson."

"What can I do for you?"

That response left Matheson a bit confused. "Well, ah, you asked to see me, Sheriff."

George Stuart was confused too. He cocked his head to one side. "I don't know—"

Footsteps sounded in the dark alley between the sheriff's office and the hardware store. Stuart's body tensed. He turned toward the noise as a red flare exploded from the darkness. Stuart staggered and tried to draw his gun. A second shot sent him tumbling down the stairway.

Matheson darted to the front of the sheriff's office and drew his Colt. There was a bright half moon in the sky, making Matheson more visible than the gunman, who was shielded by the darkness of the alley. Matheson listened carefully but heard nothing. The gunman hadn't run off. Maybe the killer wasn't sure that his job was done. Sheriff George Stuart could still be alive.

A man the decent people of a town depended on for protection now lay bleeding at the bottom of a stairway. Matheson suddenly wondered who would care if he died that night. No one. And why should they? The west had plenty of hired guns.

Boyd decided on a foolish course of action he would have scorned only a few weeks before. He would use himself as bait to draw the gunman's fire. He holstered the Colt and, pretending to believe that his adversary was gone, ran toward the fallen sheriff.

He heard a slight shifting of feet, dropped to the boardwalk, and drew his gun as another flame tore through the darkness. Matheson's first shot was followed by scrambling footsteps; his second shot hit something—the wooden wall of the hardware store. "You can't hit what you can't see," Boyd muttered to himself.

Matheson sprang to his feet. The gunman seemed to be really gone. Or was it gunmen? The frantic running sounds Matheson heard seemed to indicate more than one killer and the shots did not sound like they came from the same gun. Boyd cautiously made his way to George Stuart's body, which lay partially on the last step of the stairway and partially on the boardwalk.

He was dead. Matheson knew it the moment he looked at him. But the gunfighter placed two fingers on Stuart's neck anyway. No pulse.

"Drop the gun and lift your hands Mister! I have a Winchester aimed right at the back of your head!"

Matheson followed the instructions. Suddenly he was surrounded by at least a half dozen men. They grabbed his .45, tied his hands behind his back, and twirled him around to face the man with the Winchester. It was Pete, one of the men Matheson had encountered at Remick's General Store that afternoon.

"Evening, Pete," Matheson said. "I see you still have some flour in your hair. Of course, that doesn't surprise me." Boyd sniffed the air. "You're obviously not a man who spends much time cleaning himself up."

Pete drove a hard fist against the side of Matheson's head. The gunfighter's captors stood back as he plunged to the ground, landing only a few feet in front of George Stuart's corpse. Matheson tried to buoy up, a task complicated by the fact that his hands were bound behind him. Before he could get to his feet, one of the surrounding men aimed a six-shooter at him and cocked the weapon.

Pete looked down at the gunfighter with a face that was red with raw hatred. "You ain't makin' a fool of me ever again." He jerked a thumb behind him to a frail, elderly man. "This here is Mayor Clarence Potts. He just appointed me actin' sheriff. I'm placin' you under arrest for the murder of George Stuart."

Chapter Five

Sheriff Pete Wheeler looked through the bars at his prisoner. He spoke with mock kindness: "Sure ya don't want no lunch? A man needs his nourishment to stand trial and all."

"I don't care for the seasoning," Matheson replied. Wheeler had conspicuously spit on the food as he carried it toward Boyd Matheson's cell.

"Now that's a real shame," Wheeler said with a malicious grin. "Because I 'spect all your grub will be seasoned the same way."

A door that separated the cell area from the office flew open. A young man that Matheson recognized from the gang that had arrested him the night before looked in anxiously at the sheriff. "Pete—" He saw the angry grimace on Wheeler's face. "I mean, Sheriff Wheeler; there's some folks here to see the prisoner."

"Tell 'em to go away!" Wheeler barked.

A deep distinguished voice boomed out from the office. "There are still laws in the Arizona Territory, Pete Wheeler, even if this town does have a crook and a coward for an acting sheriff. Let us see the prisoner or I'll make so much trouble Bull Grady will find himself a new serf to do the king's bidding!"

Another grimace ran across Wheeler's face, but this time it was mingled with frustration and worry. The sheriff stalked out of the cell area, the lunch tray still in his hand. Boyd listened as Pete Wheeler began an angry, intense conversation with the newcomers.

The closed door made it impossible to hear what was being said. The sheriff's office contained four large jail cells and Matheson stared at the empty cell across from him. He didn't want to die. That was a strange feeling. For years, he had taken on dangerous jobs with a numb indifference as to whether or not he survived. But now Boyd Matheson felt he had to live. There were important tasks he needed to get done.

Matheson laughed out loud at his own reasoning. He hadn't done anything worthwhile with his life since Ann died, twelve years ago. What made him think he could start now?

The door to the jail area opened again and Perkins began yapping as he ran to the gunfighter. Boyd crouched down and petted the dog as best as he could through the iron bars. "Hello there, fella. It's good to know I have at least one friend in this town."

"You have more than one friend, Mr. Matheson." Laurel Remick's voice was as melodic as ever. Boyd gave the mutt a final pat on the head then stood back up.

"Miss Remick, you shouldn't—"

"Grandfather and I heard about what happened." The young woman's face was tight with tension. "We got one of the most respected men in this town to defend you, Reverend Frank Stuben."

Laurel gestured to her left where a man who stood at slightly under five feet smiled benignly at her, then turned to face Matheson. "Laurel Remick is a fine young lady who is much too polite to tell you the name everyone calls me. I'm Reverend Stubby, Mr. Matheson, and I'll do everything I can to help you."

Matheson tried not to show it but he was a bit stunned by the reverend. He had certainly seen short people before but none with the deep, cultured voice of Reverend Stubby.

"Let me tell you a little about myself," Reverend Stubby said. "I was born just outside of this town, the last of nine kids. My mother called me the runt of the litter and she was right. My older brothers used to amuse themselves by beating up on me. That probably stunted what little opportunity I had for growth. About the time I was eleven, my mother packed me off to a cousin of hers who lived in the east. She told me I needed to get an education because I was incapable of doing honest work.

"Well, I proved her wrong. In the east I cleaned floors, cleaned walls and cleaned other things that are not proper to mention in the presence of a lady."

Boyd glanced at Laurel. A wry smile played across her lips as she listened to Reverend Stubby. "I guess I got a little carried away with my cleaning because I got it in my head that what really needed cleaning was the souls of men. I studied for the ministry then came right back here and started Gradyville's first church."

"Bull Grady didn't like that one bit," Laurel said. "But Reverend—" She looked at the parson, who gave her a friendly smile. "Reverend Stubby started the church anyway. And he didn't stop there! He organized the town council and now he's running against Clarence Potts for mayor."

Matheson snapped his fingers and pointed at the parson. "You must be the pulpit pounder Grady was complaining about."

The parson laughed out loud. "Bull Grady has called me a lot worse things." Reverend Stubby's demeanor suddenly turned serious. "I'm not going to sweeten anything for you, Mr. Matheson. You are in a lot of trouble. Bull Grady just had the sheriff murdered. The Remicks told me what you did for them. They admire you and so do I. But, let me assure you, Bull Grady is not one of your admirers. He plans to frame you for the killing and he's got the power to do it. I want you to tell me everything that happened to you yesterday from the moment you rode into town."

As Boyd told his story he found himself assessing

the very unusual individual who stood on the other side of the bars from him. Reverend Stubby had a normal sized head which appeared a bit too big for his small body. His thick black hair was lightly salted with gray.

The gunfighter wondered what life must be like for such an extraordinary man trapped in such a limited body. The pastor was a man of obvious courage to go against Bull Grady and his thugs. Boyd found himself gaining a great deal of respect for the man called Reverend Stubby.

"They're planning to hold your trial tonight in the Fighting Bull Saloon," Laurel said. "This town grabs whatever entertainment it can. I'm afraid you've become an attraction, Mr. Matheson."

"It gets worse," Reverend Stubby added. "The prosecutor will be Jeb Crane, the only lawyer in town."

"If Crane is the only lawyer, then who is presiding as judge?" Boyd asked.

Laurel closed her eyes and spoke in a whisper. "Bull Grady."

"What?"

The parson nodded his head. "Years ago, Grady used his influence to get appointed as a judge."

Matheson looked at the ceiling for a moment, then back at his companions. "There's another reason for holding this trial at night, isn't there? It would be easy to claim that after a guilty verdict was rendered, a crowd of good citizens decided to dispense justice quickly and carried the guilty party to a nearby tree."

Reverend Stubby nodded his head. "The whole town knows what Bull Grady is up to. I've got to convince them they can stand up to that man."

"You've already convinced some people of that, Parson," Laurel said. "That's what the town council is all about."

Reverend Stubby smiled at the young woman as if he considered her statement a bit naive. "Our town council isn't very big," he said, turning to Matheson. "There's the Remicks and a few other merchants, along with Doc Evans."

"This town has a doctor?" Boyd tried to sound casual. He had been thinking about visiting a sawbones for some time.

"We do on most days before four in the afternoon," the parson answered in a sad manner. "Then the drink begins to take over Doc Rufus Evans." An idea seemed to hit Reverend Stubby. "I should go see Rufus right now! The doc may have some important evidence for us. He's got to stay sober."

The reverend easily slipped his right hand between the bars of Matheson's cell and shook hands with the prisoner. "It's an honor to represent you, Sir," Reverend Stubby said. "Don't worry about paying me. I discovered a long time ago that a parson in the west works for other than monetary rewards. There's a dear lady in my congregation who is always proclaiming that the preacher should be the poorest in the church. There is no biblical basis for her opinion but it is still one that is shared by many at The First Church of

Gradyville. They insist that my rewards will be in eternity. Well, okay. Right now, my job is to ensure that Mr. Boyd Matheson doesn't arrive in eternity too soon!"

Boyd and Laurel watched as Reverend Stubby strode out of the cell area. "I hope he finds that doctor in time," Matheson said wistfully.

Laurel Remick gave him a smile that looked wonderful even through iron bars. "I wasn't just talking big about Reverend Stubby. Don't let . . ."

"The west has plenty of tall men with muscles," Matheson interrupted, "but not enough men of strong character. There are never enough of those. The parson sure has sand. I just hope that helping me won't get him in deeper trouble with Bull Grady."

The smile left Laurel's face. Matheson was sorry to see it go. "You're right, Mr. Matheson, there are plenty of strong men in the west, but not enough men of character. Bull Grady has most of the strong men on his payroll. Grady is opposed by people like Reverend Stubby and my grandfather. They have courage, but not the physical strength to back it up."

Laurel looked away for a moment and wiped a hand over her face. When she turned back tears were still visible in her eyes. "The sheriff was the only powerful man on our side. And they ambushed him!" The tears increased. This time, the young woman didn't try to stop them. "Bull Grady plans to kill you, Mr. Matheson. Hanging you will solve all his problems. He can report that the sheriff was murdered by a . . . a gunfighter who was tried and hanged. It'll all look so neat and proper on paper. The rangers won't come near."

"Have you or your grandfather tried to contact the rangers?"

"Yes, but it's useless." Laurel crossed her arms in front of her as if she were suffering a chill. "We're so out of the way here. The rangers remember Bull Grady the way he was years ago. A builder. A person who takes care of matters. He used to be difficult, but not too unfair. The rangers don't realize what Bull Grady has become."

Boyd gripped the unyielding bars that imprisoned him. "Miss Remick, this may sound strange coming from a man who—well a man like me, but I hate the Bull Gradys of this world. If I get out of this jail I'll do everything I can to stop him."

Laurel's voice dropped to a whisper. "I know that's true, Mr. Matheson. But you must not speak of yourself in a bad way. As far as I'm concerned, you are the man who rescued my grandfather and me when no one else would come. I hope and pray that you get out of this mess . . . alive."

An uneasy silence settled over them as if they both felt something important needed to be said, but couldn't figure out what it was. Finally, Laurel reached over, gently squeezed Matheson's hand and then hurried away with Perkins scampering behind her.

She had been gone for a few minutes when the gunfighter caught himself rolling a cigarette. It would be the fourth cigarette he had smoked since being in prison. Matheson's hands trembled and this time it wasn't an act. Jail made it impossible for him to take his mind off tobacco. There was nowhere to go, nothing to do for diversion.

He had coughed a bit over the third cigarette but the gunfighter convinced himself that, if he smoked it slowly, a fourth cigarette wouldn't do him any harm.

At first, he seemed to be right. It wasn't until he was half way through the smoke when, suddenly, an iron chain seemed to wrap around his chest. He gasped for air and tried not to cough. A dizziness hit and Matheson dropped to his knees. He crawled toward the far corner of the cell away from the office. He didn't want anyone to hear the coughing that he could no longer contain. Matheson's body went into convulsions as he lay on the floor and tried to cough silently.

When the spell had passed, he looked toward the office. The door was still closed. That meant no one had heard him. Otherwise, they would have rushed in to watch. Like Laurel had said, people grab whatever entertainment they can.

Sucking in air like a drowning man who had just surfaced, the gunfighter crawled to his cot and lay down on it. After a while his breathing became normal and he felt better. He vowed that he would never smoke again.

Then the gunfighter laughed bitterly. Later tonight, a rope might help him to keep that vow.

Chapter Six

Matheson sat beside Reverend Stubby at a new but poorly made table. He surveyed the scene inside the Fighting Bull Saloon. There would be no poker games played here tonight. All the round tables had been removed and replaced by rows of chairs. Every one of those chairs was filled, mostly by people who were strangers to Matheson. A pleasant exception was the row directly behind him where Laurel Remick sat with Cassius Remick beside her and Perkins lying at her feet.

There was another familiar face in the Fighting Bull. Clay Adams stood behind the last row of chairs, directly beside the saloon's swinging doors. The young man appeared very interested in what was going on, but at the same time, seemed to want to distance himself from the proceedings.

To the left of the defense table was the prosecution. Boyd observed that the prosecutor, Jeb Crane, was a red-haired, red-bearded man of about forty-five.

The jury was to the left of the prosecution table, where twelve chairs had been hastily assembled. At that moment, the Fighting Bull's bar was still open and the members of the jury were bustling back and forth exchanging jokes with the barkeep and each other in preparation for deciding whether a man lived or died.

Reverend Stubby observed Boyd's interest in the jury. "I'm very happy with our twelve civic-minded citizens."

"How did you and the prosecutor manage to agree on the twelve jury members?" Matheson whispered.

Reverend Stubby's smile could almost be called devilish. "Mr. Jeb Crane, our town's only barrister, comes from Boston. I informed him that I had heard stories about him while attending school in that fine city. I also mentioned that I had written certain authorities in Boston regarding his activities and had received some interesting replies. Mr. Crane was cooperative in selecting a jury."

"Exactly what did Crane do that made him leave Boston?" Boyd asked.

That smile expanded. "I don't know. I attended school in Boston. The rest of it was lies." The pastor chortled, then took on a more serious demeanor. "Scripture generally condemns lying, but it is justified under certain circumstances. Rahab lied to save the lives of spies from Israel. Joshua 2:4. I lied to save your life."

Boyd could only shake his head and glance at the ceiling. He knew from reading newspapers that some cities in the east now required that a trial have at least three men who qualified as lawyers: the judge, the prosecutor and the defense attorney. Boyd reckoned it would be a while before the west got that civilized. What was going on now in Gradyville reminded him of the many miner's courts he had seen in small settlements throughout Arizona and Colorado.

In front of the bar sat a massive desk and chair which the gunfighter recognized. They came from Bull Grady's office. A gavel now lay on top of the desk. Pete Wheeler suddenly entered the saloon area from a door beside the bar. He gave a hand signal of some kind to the bartender then shouted over the babble that filled the Fighting Bull. "Everone be quiet! Finish your drinkin'. The bar is now closed. There will be no drinkin' or jawin' when court is, ah, ah . . ."

"In session," Jeb Crane whispered sharply from the prosecution table.

"When court is in session," Wheeler shouted. "Now, all rise, Judge Grady is comin'."

The side door opened again and Bull Grady charged into the room as everyone dutifully stood up. Matheson couldn't help thinking that, yes, Grady did resemble an old bull. The judge walked directly to his desk and stood behind the chair. "I will remind you people that this room is now a court of law!" Grady's voice had a natural boom. He didn't have to shout. "All gents will take their hats off. Ladies will make sure their handbags are held in a manner that will insure they don't fall to the floor during court proceedings. You may be seated."

"Isn't the judge supposed to sit first?" Boyd asked Reverend Stubby as they returned to their chairs.

"Yes," the parson nodded toward Grady. "But sitting down is an undertaking for Bull Grady. He wants everyone to be fussing over their hats and handbags and not watching him."

The parson spoke without mockery. He had genuine sympathy for Grady's physical problems. Boyd noted that Grady did not return the kindness. The defense table ran across the top of Reverend Stubby's chest, making him look a bit silly.

"Is the prosecution ready?" Grady asked.

Jeb Crane buoyed up and down with a quick, "We are, your honor."

Grady's voice took on a mildly irritated tone as he turned to Reverend Stubby. "Is the defense ready?"

Frank Stuben jumped onto the defense table. "Indeed we are! But before we begin I would like to thank the court for providing the defense with what must be the tallest table in all of the Arizona Territory!"

The judged glowered at Reverend Stubby who was smiling benignly at him from atop the table. "It is not the fault of the court if your chin scrapes the table." A few guffaws could be heard from the crowd.

Reverend Stubby kept his smile and robust voice. "I am most happy and gratified to hear that, Your Honor."

"What do you mean?"

Keeping his position on the tabletop, the pastor smiled at the spectators, then returned his gaze to the bench. "What you said was absolutely true, Your Honor. You have nothing to do with the fact that I am short. That matter was decided by the Lord Himself, maker of heaven and earth. Now, in recent years, Your Honor has, on occasion, confused himself with God. I am most encouraged to hear that you have finally erased that confusion from your mind."

This time the courtroom erupted in laughter. Bull Grady angrily pounded his gavel, then barked at the prosecutor, "Get on with your opening statement!"

Reverend Stubby hopped off the table. As he sat down, he whispered to his client: "Crane will tell the jury they better find you guilty if they know what's good for them."

That's exactly what happened. Crane's opening statement was crammed with remarks like, "Boyd Matheson has committed a crime against all of Grady-ville. A crime for which he must hang if this town, including you twelve gentlemen, is ever to know peace again."

Reverend Stubby fired back with a strong rebuttal. "History is filled with examples of tyrants who thought they were above the law. Tyrants who crumbled when enough people got fed up and refused to take any more. I urge you gentlemen to decide this case on the basis of evidence. Tell the world that Gradyville is a town that is ruled by law, not by a despot!"

Jeb Crane called the first witness. "Our distinguished mayor, Mr. Clarence Potts."

After the elderly man had been sworn in, Jeb Crane spoke to him in a deferential voice. This was a very important official whose word on anything should be the last word. "Mr. Mayor, I know you can clear this whole matter up for us in short time. Would you tell us what you witnessed last night?"

"Well, I'm workin' late in the store."

"Just for the record, you mean your hardware store, the one that is right next door to the sheriff's office?"

"That's right. The store is closed, of course. I'm, ah, doin' bookeepin' and things, you know . . ."

"Yes," Crane smiled graciously at the spectators and then at the jury. "I'm sure we're all aware that a successful businessman must often work far beyond business hours. Please continue, Mr. Mayor."

"Well, my eyes is gettin' a bit heavy, so I steps outside for a little fresh air."

"And what did you see?" Jeb Crane asked.

The mayor raised and pointed a bony finger. "That man, Boyd Matheson, he's standin' in front of the sheriff's office. George Stuart comes out onto the stairway from his livin' quarters above the office. Without sayin' nothin', Matheson pulls out his gun and shoots twice. Both bullets hit the sheriff and he rolls down the stairs."

Jeb Crane pressed his lips together in a grim manner, then walked to the prosecution's table and picked up a gun. "Mr. Mayor, do you recognize this?"

"Course," Clarence replied. "That'd be a Colt .45. The one Matheson used to kill the sheriff. The walnut handle is sorta an unusual color. Not many like it 'round here."

Jeb Crane nodded approvingly. "Your honor, the prosecution will submit this gun as evidence." He dropped the Colt on the edge of Grady's desk, then continued. "So, Boyd Matheson draws his Colt .45 and murders the sheriff in cold blood. What did he do next?"

"Matheson jumps to the ground and fires a shot into the side of my hardware store."

"Did you know why he did that?" Crane asked.

"At first, no, but soon I gets it figured," the mayor spoke quickly. "He's settin' up some crazy alibi about a gunman killin' the sheriff from the alley and how he tried to stop him."

Reverend Stubby jumped to his feet. "Your Honor—"

"Be quiet!" Grady boomed.

"But Your Honor, I object!"

"You're not behind a pulpit, Stubby. Sit down and be quiet!"

The parson's voice suddenly became good natured. "I apologize to the court, Your Honor. For a moment I forgot that Gradyville is the only territory in the west ruled by a king."

There was a scattering of laughter. Bull Grady started to pound his gavel, then settled for snapping at the prosecutor, "Get on with the questions!"

Jeb Crane straightened his string tie, even though it wasn't crooked. "Now, Mr. Mayor, could you tell the court what happened after Matheson fired into the side of your store?"

"Well, fortunately, Pete Wheeler and a few other boys be in the area and hears the shots. They come runnin'. I appoints Pete actin' sheriff and orders him to arrest the killer."

Jeb Crane cleared his throat nervously. Reverend Stubby gave both the prosecutor and the witness a long, curious stare then whispered to his client, "If you think the lies have been bad up till now, I think they're about to spring a real whopper."

His throat fully cleared, Crane continued, "Mr. Mayor, had Sheriff Stuart ever discussed Boyd Matheson with you?"

"Yes." Clarence Potts paused; he seemed to be mentally rehearsing his speech one more time. "George Stuart tells me he tangles with Matheson a few years back. He says Matheson vows to kill him someday."

"That's a lie!" Laurel Remick was on her feet. "George Stuart never confided in Clarence Potts. He knew the mayor couldn't be trusted. The mayor is Bull Grady's puppet. Everyone knows that."

An explosion of shouts and curses bellowed through the saloon as Cassius Remick gently placed a hand on his granddaughter's shoulder and motioned for her to sit back down. Bull Grady pounded the gavel on his desk, then fired the word "silence" over the chaos in front of him. Voices dropped to a low whisper. The big man glared across the room and even the whispering ceased. For the first time, Matheson realized the extent of the fear Bull Grady had instilled in the townsfolk.

Grady continued to stare at the crowd while saying not a word. The atmosphere in the saloon became increasingly tense. Some people actually felt grateful when Grady turned to Jeb Crane and spoke. "You got any more to say?"

The attorney smiled anxiously. "No, Your Honor. The testimony of our town's distinguished mayor has established, beyond a doubt, that the defendant, Boyd Matheson, gunned down Sheriff George Stuart in a brutal act of revenge. There is no more that needs to be said. The prosecution rests its case." Crane returned to his chair.

"Your turn, Stubby." The judge spoke without looking in the direction of the defense table.

"Thank you, Your Honor." Frank Stuben replied cheerfully as he approached the witness. "Clarence, how's business at the hardware store?"

"The store is prosperin'."

"That's not really surprising," the reverend continued to speak in a friendly banter, "seeing how you own the only hardware store in Gradyville. Of course, it wasn't always that way, right Clarence?"

Clarence Potts shifted his position on the witness chair. "Don't know what ya mean."

The friendly tone left Reverend Stubby's voice. "Remember Riley Collins and his wife, Sarah?"

The skin on the mayor's face seemed to tighten. He pursed his lips before he spoke. "Young fools! Imagine, strangers to this town, tryin' to open a store."

"Some folks thought the Collins did a fine job with their hardware store." The reverend turned his face to the jury. "As I recall, they took some business away from you."

"Nothin' that amounts to anythin'." Clarence shifted forward in his chair. "They gets what they deserve!"

"And who gave them what they deserved, Clarence? Who burned down their store?" As Reverend Stubby asked the questions he shot an accusing glance toward Bull Grady. The judge shifted backward in his chair, then looked at his desk.

Watching the exchange, Boyd Matheson realized the two men were in a ferocious struggle for the soul of the town, and he was caught in the middle. The pastor was winning a very minor skirmish, but hard battles lay ahead.

Guttural sounds came from Clarence's throat. He finally spoke in a wavering voice. "Don't know. The fools probably knocks over a lamp or somethin'.

Reverend Stubby looked around the saloon, then spoke in a low voice. "And how do you account for the bullets that were found in the Collins' bodies, after they were dragged out of the ashes?"

Jeb Crane jumped to his feet. "You honor, I object to—"

"I withdraw the question." The clergyman looked at the jury then back at Clarence Potts. "A few days after Sarah and Riley were murdered, you suddenly became interested in serving the community, didn't you Clarence?"

"Don't know what yer talkin' 'bout."

"The day after the Collins' were buried, you announced you were running for mayor. Bull Grady paid for your campaign and, no doubt, paid for a large number of your votes."

Suppressed chortles bobbed in the air. Judge Grady picked up his gavel, then tossed it back to the desk in disgust.

"Thank you Mr. Mayor, I have no further questions." The parson turned and walked back to the defense table. Clarence Potts sputtered nervous words to himself as he left the witness chair. Bull Grady noticed that even some of his supporters were fidgeting nervously over the memories of Sarah and Riley.

"You calling any witnesses, Stubby?" Grady almost shouted.

"Yes, Your Honor. I would like to call Dr. Rufus Evans."

The judge smiled in a slow, cruel manner. "Rufus Evans please approach the bench and be sworn in. Or should I have some of my boys carry the good doctor to the bench?"

Laughter filled the saloon. This time, Bull Grady laughed with the crowd.

But not for long. Reverend Stubby again jumped up on the defense table. He waited for the laughter to subside, then spoke. "I am pleased to inform the court that Dr. Evans is perfectly sober and Your Honor can accept the credit for our doctor's sobriety."

Reverend Stubby beamed a smile at Bull Grady, then returned his eyes to the spectators. "All of us know that Doc Evans has a problem with the drink. And we also know that Bull Grady owns every saloon in this town and he has been watering down that cheap rotgut he serves, more and more with each passing day. The situation has gotten to the point where it now takes Doc Evans, and other folks who like their drink, a good day and a half of imbibing just to get respectably drunk."

Bull Grady was again on the wrong side of the laughter. He didn't try to silence the spectators, but sat and looked at Reverend Stubby with an intense hatred.

Boyd Matheson wasn't laughing either. He was studying Rufus Evans as the doctor came forward and was sworn in. Evans was a tall man who walked with a stoop and was thin to the point of looking skeletal. His dark hair was generously laced with white. After what was said about the doctor in court, Matheson wasn't surprised by the red veins which streaked Evans' nose and upper cheeks.

But Rufus Evans was not drunk on this night. He was tense and maybe scared. Matheson looked at Reverend Stubby and saw the hard determination in his eyes. The testimony of Dr. Rufus Evans would decide this case.

The pastor approached the witness chair slowly, his voice a bit lower than normal. "Rufus, where were you last night?"

"I was at home," the doctor paused, "I was . . . reading."

Reverend Stubby's voice remained hushed. "Did anything unusual happen?"

Rufus Evans gave a bitter laugh. "A good man was brought to me—dead. Nothing much unusual about that."

"The man's name?"

"George Stuart. He had been shot twice."

Reverend Stubby raised his voice slightly. "Did you remove any bullets from Sheriff Stuart's body?"

"I did . . ."

"And do you have one of those bullets with you now?"

"I do." The doctor reached into the pocket of his frock coat and brought out a bullet.

"Rufus, how long have you been a doctor?" Reverend Stubby asked.

"I finished medical school right before the war."

"And you served as a doctor during the war between the states?"

Rufus Evans' lips trembled but no sounds came out. The doctor finally managed to wheeze a "yes" which sounded like a dying man's final breath.

"After the war, you came out west and, in time, established a practice here in Gradyville."

"That's correct."

Reverend Stubby looked directly at the jury and then continued. "Between serving in the war and being a doctor in the west, I suspect you have pulled bullets from many men."

This time Doc Evans didn't pause; anger laced his voice. "Yes Reverend, I have taken bullets out of many men and, for that matter, I've had to treat bullet wounds for more than a few women and children."

Reverend Stubby again raised his voice. "Doctor Evans, could you tell me what caliber of gun that bullet in your hand came from?"

"It came from a Navy .38."

The courtroom sounded like a saloon again as shouts, loud chattering and even laughter rebounded off the walls. No one paid much attention to the pounding of Bull Grady's gavel. Jeb Crane jumped to his feet and was trying to make an objection when Reverend Stubby grabbed the Colt .45 from the edge of Grady's desk. He lifted the gun over his head, stretching his arm to its fullest possible length.

The clergyman's voice fired through the raucous confusion in front of him. "Doctor Evans, is there any way that bullet you pulled from George Stuart could have come from Boyd Matheson's Colt .45?"

"No way at all!" The doctor shouted.

Jeb Crane tried to yell above the hullabaloo. "Your Honor, I must—"

"Sustained!" Bull Grady pounded his gavel again, this time with more effect. The saloon once again came close to resembling a courtroom. Grady lifted the gavel and pointed it at his enemy. "You won't say one more word about that bullet."

Stubby ignored the judge and turned to his witness. "What about the other shot that hit George Stuart? Did it come from a Navy .38?"

"No."

"Could you tell us the caliber of pistol it did come from?"

"It didn't come from a pistol. The other shot came from a rifle, something like a Henry .44 would be my guess."

A scattering of incredulous whispers sounded across the saloon; otherwise there was silence. Reverend Stubby took advantage of the lull. He jumped onto the defense table and addressed the crowd. "All of you now know what really happened in our town last night!" The pastor's eyes flared with the same intensity that filled his voice. "George Stuart was butchered in a cowardly ambush. Everyone knows our sheriff ate dinner alone most nights in his room above the office. Right after dinner he would do a round. Last night two men were waiting in the alley between the sheriff's office and the hardware store. Someone told Boyd Matheson that the sheriff wanted to see him. Had the sheriff left the office too soon one of the two men in the alley would have jawed with him till Matheson got there."

Jeb Crane was on his feet. "Your Honor, I must object to this disgraceful—"

Reverend Stubby shifted his gaze to the prosecutor. Crane looked away and then slowly sat down. Boyd Matheson knew the charade of a trial had come to an end and a much more deadly contest was beginning.

The pastor continued, his voice sharp with judgment and condemnation. "But Matheson appeared just when they wanted him to, as the sheriff was stepping out of his office. The two men shot down George Stuart and ran. Then using our honorable mayor as a pawn, a plan was launched to frame Boyd Matheson for the murder—"

"That's a lie!" Jeb Crane was standing up and shouting.

"Everyone knows where the lies are coming from!" the pastor retorted. "Only the lies aren't even good lies! Bull Grady and his men hold you people in such contempt, they don't even bother to create false evidence. Either that or Bull Grady can't tell the difference between a Henry Rifle and a Colt .45!"

Matheson saw the almost monstrous figure of Bull Grady bolt from his chair and charge toward Reverend Stubby.

"Look out!" Matheson was on his feet facing Grady. Chairs squeaked and Laurel screamed as two men grabbed Matheson from behind. Grady smashed a fist against the side of the clergyman's head, whirling him off the table and onto the floor. Cries and loud curses resounded throughout the saloon. Matheson plunged an elbow into the midriff of one of his captors, who jackknifed onto his knees. Matheson used the freed arm to land a punch into the right eye of the other captor who staggered backward three steps.

"Grab him!"

Matheson landed a haymaker on the next man who charged at him. As the attacker hit the floor, another man jumped on Matheson's back. The gunfighter crouched, grabbed the arm that was beginning to coil around his neck and flipped the weight off his back. Two other men grabbed Matheson's arms and a third slammed a fist against the right side of his face.

Through blurred vision, Matheson saw Cassius Remick charging toward him to help. Pete Wheeler pushed the old man to the floor and was about to kick him.

"STOP IT!" The young, feminine voice caused a startled hush in the Fighting Bull Saloon.

Laurel Remick was helping Reverend Stubby to his feet. The pastor began to walk around, but his gait was unsteady.

Laurel turned to the barkeeper. "We need two glasses of water, one for Reverend Stuben and one for my grandfather."

The barkeep did nothing.

"Bring the water now!" Laurel shouted.

The barkeeper's footsteps could be heard throughout the saloon as the crowd stood in silence and watched him deliver the two glasses of water. Matheson noticed that Cassius Remick scrambled back up quickly and didn't appear seriously hurt. He quickly shifted his gaze to Reverend Stubby. After a sip of water, the clergyman appeared more steady.

Laurel glared at the barkeeper who kept his eyes away from hers as he hustled back behind the bar. "What do you know," she shouted sarcastically, "a man who can actually pour two glasses of water without first getting permission from Bull Grady."

Nervous laughter tittered in the saloon. The young woman didn't join in. Her face was filled with scorn. "There's no more than a handful of men in this town who deserve to be called men. The rest of you are cowards, good for nothing but licking your master's boots!"

"Shut up!" The angry response came from a male voice somewhere in the crowd.

"You want me to shut up? Then come here and tell me that face to face!" Laurel glared across the room, then continued. "That's what I thought. You don't have the sand to look me in the eye. These days, it looks like most of the men in this town don't have enough sand to fill a thimble."

Laurel paused. She had the attention of everyone in the saloon. Even Bull Grady, who had retreated behind his desk, stood watching her, his mouth twitching slightly.

"It starts with letting one bully push you around," Laurel continued. "Then, before you know it you're scared. Scared all the time. Scared to stand up for what you know is right. The pastor doesn't have much in the way of size, and my grandfather is old, but they amount to a lot more than most of the men in this saloon. And that goes double for you weasels who work for Grady." Laurel looked down at Perkins, who was wagging his tail with a worried look in his eyes. "My dog has more sense than to fetch a stick thrown by Bull Grady. What does that say about you so-called men who work for that tyrant?"

A confused rumble of hushed conversations followed Laurel's question. Matheson noticed Clay Adams, now standing only a few yards away from Laurel. He was listening intently, his face ashen, his eyes darting with indecision.

Bull Grady wanted to order Laurel Remick killed where she stood, but he knew such an act would turn the town against him and bring down his empire. When he spoke his voice had a good-natured, mocking quality to it.

"My, my, Cassius, that granddaughter of yours does give a fancy speech. 'Course, if she spent more time in that rundown store, stocking shelves and what not, instead of giving fool speeches, maybe you could afford to pay your rent now and again."

There was some laughter in the Fighting Bull, mostly from Grady's men. Bull Grady hadn't regained complete control of the situation yet and knew it.

"So, the little girl thinks I'm a tyrant. Well, now, let's just get us some democracy. I hereby appoint every gent in this saloon to the jury. As a reward for your civic duty there will be free drinks served to every jury member!"

Raucous cheers exploded across the saloon followed by laughter and a scrambling toward the bar. Grady smiled broadly and held up one hand, the crowd became quiet again. "All you gents heard the evidence presented here tonight. I'm ordering Sheriff Wheeler to take the prisoner back to jail. After you honorable members of the jury wet your whistles you can decide among yourselves what should be done with the killer!"

The shouts became louder. A half dozen men, led by Wheeler, circled around Matheson. Bull Grady quickly conferred with another group, then disappeared through a side door while the men began to carry his desk and chair back upstairs to his office.

Reverend Stubby watched Wheeler and several other owlhoots push Matheson through the swinging doors, then did a quick look around the saloon. The mood was getting very ugly. A large number of men were at the bar anxiously partaking of false courage. The pastor laughed bitterly to himself as he watched several of the town's upstanding, good citizens quickly exit the Fighting Bull and disappear into the night.

"We've got to do something, they're going to hang Mr. Matheson!"

Reverend Stubby shook off his private thoughts and looked up into Laurel's moist eyes. "Yes, but we have some time." He nodded toward the bar. "Our honorable jury seems to be in no real hurry. They will require plenty of libation before they take Matheson out to the cottonwood. We're going to get there first."

A small group began to huddle around Laurel and the clergyman. They were all members of the town council: Doc Evans, Cassius Remick, Hank and Orin Mellor. The Mellors were father and son and owned the town's only livery stable. They had purchased the stable after an explosion at the mine had ended their working days as miners.

"Don't mind Grady, Miss Laurel," Hank, the older Mellor, said angrily. "You spoke good and you spoke what's true."

"I wasn't talking about you and Orin—"

"I heard some o' the jawin' as gents were leavin' the saloon," Orin said. "Talkin' about how they'd like to do more but got a wife and kids to think about." Orin shook his head. "Pa raised five kids and I saw to it that he has three grandkids. We know 'bout families. That's why we've got to fight Bull Grady. We don't want kids growin' up in a town ruled by the likes of him!"

Hank pressed his lips together, then spoke firmly. "We'll do everthing we can do, Reverend!"

Reverend Stubby nodded thanks to the two men. Hank's left arm was withered and Orin walked with a limp, both disabilities a result of the mining explosion. The pastor wondered if their physical impediments hadn't pushed the Mellors to do more with their lives, to be better men. He wondered if that very same thing wasn't true of himself.

The pastor's thoughts quickly shifted to the young man standing several feet behind the Mellors. Clay Adams was watching the conspirators. The conflict that Reverend Stubby, like his client, had seen in the young man's eyes earlier, now raged more fiercely.

"We'll meet in fifteen minutes behind Cassius' store," the pastor spoke in a firm whisper. Clay Adams took a couple steps closer to the group. "From there we can take a back trail out to the big cottonwood. We'll wait for them on that small knoll just past the tree."

"How . . ." Laurel had started to talk in a normal voice. When she saw the men at the bar glance in her direction, she lowered the volume. "How can you be so sure they'll take Mr. Matheson to the big cotton-wood?"

"Every hanging in Gradyville, legal or otherwise, has taken place there," Reverend Stubby said. "But you're right. We can't gamble. That's why I want you to stay here in town and keep your ears open. If you find out they have other ideas beside the cottonwood, come get us—fast."

Laurel nodded her head.

"We all know what we have to do."

Reverend Stubby's voice had a clarion sound to it. The group quickly dispersed. Clay Adams didn't move. He watched as Laurel Remick left the saloon with her grandfather, Perkins scrambling between them.

"Tonight you'll be riding with me. It's important that you do exactly what I tell you."

Clay Adams looked down into the pastor's intense gaze. He took a step backward. "Don't know what you're talkin'—"

Rowdy laughter scorched over the saloon. A voice from the bar shouted, "This har juree finds the defendant guilty as sin!" More laughter followed.

Reverend Stubby glanced at the revelers, then looked accusingly at Clay Adams. "You know exactly what I mean! You heard what the girl said and you know every word was the truth. Now, are you willing to stand against Bull Grady?"

Adams held up both hands in a stop gesture. "Look here, I jus' work for Grady . . ."

Reverend Stubby took two steps toward the young man, pointing a finger at him. The pastor's voice was still a whisper but Clay Adams had no trouble hearing it.

"You can't hide behind that kind of talk any longer. The lines are drawn. Are you going to stand with a killer or are you going to stand for the truth?"

Chapter Seven

Clay Adams was terrified. He rode hard to stay abreast of the strange, small man who sat atop a boy's saddle. Adams felt trapped by his own stupidity. He was defying a Goliath and throwing in with a band of misfits Bull Grady could crush like they were ashes from his cigar.

Adams took his mother to church every week and knew all about Goliath being defeated by a shepherd boy. The way Clay saw it, that was a fluke not likely to be repeated in Gradyville.

As the group galloped toward the knoll, Adams realized he was doing what he had to. He had conned himself into believing Grady was a hard but fair man. But Grady had murdered the sheriff and was having an innocent man hanged for the crime.

Still, he cringed as he thought about what Bull

Grady did to traitors. He might die on this night along with Boyd Matheson.

As the band galloped up the knoll, Clay noted that the pastor might sit on a boy's saddle but he sure didn't ride like a boy. Reverend Stubby led the group into a patch of thin trees at the top of the hill, then motioned with his hand for everyone to stop.

"This should provide all the cover we need," Stubby said. "We'll be able to see them coming, but they won't see us."

A bright slab of moon cut a harsh light against a dark sky. The cottonwood seemed to stand in the middle of the light.

Orin Mellor caressed the rifle in the scabbard of his saddle. "We'll kill enough of that mob to free Matheson."

"No!" The pastor's voice was firm. "This operation will be typical Bull Grady."

"What are you gettin' at?" When Clay Adams spoke the other five men looked at him immediately. Adams realized that except for Reverend Stubby the other members of the town council did not trust him. He reckoned that he couldn't blame them.

"Bull Grady likes to keep his hands clean," Reverend Stubby replied as he patted the neck of his buckskin. "We will be dealing with boozed up miners and merchants. There will only be a few of Grady's men along to make sure Boyd Matheson keeps his appointment with a rope."

"But—" Orin again placed a hand on his rifle.

"Fire into the air! Only shoot to kill in self defense!" There was an iron in the clergyman's voice Clay Adams had not heard before.

"What are you plannin'?" Cassius Remick asked.

"I'm going to wait in those trees down by the stream." Reverend Stubby nodded downwards to his left. "When the mob arrives don't do anything until I start shooting. Then come down this hill with your guns firing. You won't have to shoot to kill."

The clergyman paused, then looked at Clay Adams. "Some men may have to die tonight. That's for me to handle."

The young man nodded.

"I better get down there." As the pastor clicked his tongue and shook his horse's reins, he noticed the town council members looking at Adams in an uneasy manner. Even Doc Evans seemed unsure about the young man. Reverend Stubby halted his buckskin and spoke to the men in a mock pious manner.

"I assume all of you gents were in church last Sunday."

There was nervous laughter.

"I'm sure you remember my sermon about Paul's conversion on the road to Damascus." Reverend Stubby's speech became slow and deliberate. "Paul was a killer. No hiding that fact. But he had a conversion and became a crusader for what was true and right. And a great crusader at that!"

Reverend Stubby paused, allowing his words to take hold, then he spoke in a low, intense whisper. "Trust me. I know a genuine conversion when I see one. Clay Adams is on our side. Now, let's do our duty!"

The clergyman moved his horse at an easy canter down the hill toward the string of trees which ran along the stream. About thirty yards away, the huge cottonwood stood regal and alone, awaiting another victim.

Clay Adams looked around at the remaining men. "What the reverend spoke was right. And I intend to prove it."

Gunshots and harsh laughter jangled from a distance. The five men tensed up as a lynch mob rode into view. Adams did a quick count.

"Eleven of them altogether," he whispered.

The mob rode toward the cottonwood in a meandering, careless manner. Clay Adams could spot only two of Grady's men; one was named Dunbar, the other was a bald-headed man everyone called Curly. Adams wasn't surprised that the two hired hands were riding next to Matheson, one on each side.

"Knew this wouldn't be easy," Adams mumbled to himself.

"Who gits the honor?" Dunbar's shout could be heard up on the knoll.

"Zeke said he'd do it." Came a reply from one of the mob.

"So, you do the honor, Zeke." This time Dunbar's shout had more force. "Toss a rope up there!" He nodded at the cottonwood. "There's a job to git done!"

"Be happy to!" Even at a distance, the five men could hear the hesitation in Zeke's voice, and the weakness in the shouts and laughter which accompanied it.

Dunbar could hear it too. An element of threat crept into his voice. "So git to it!"

Zeke took the rope from his saddle and rode slowly toward the cottonwood. As he did, a quiet came over the mob and several men moved their horses back a few steps away from the tree.

The quiet was broken by a series of shots followed by the frantic neighing of horses. Spurts of dust erupted near the lynch mob. Panicked shouts filled the air as two men abandoned the mob and went galloping back toward town.

Curly pulled out his six-shooter and tried to prevent any further desertions. "Over there." His shout had the sound of an order. "The shots are comin' from those trees by the stream."

Curly fired in the direction of the stream. The other men began to follow his lead.

Another series of shots fired down like shooting stars from the top of the knoll. Five riders galloped down the hill at a fast pace, fire and smoke exploding from their guns.

"Let's get outta here!" Three more men in the lynch mob broke away in a frenzy of panic and began riding back to town.

"Stay and fight!" Dunbar's words stopped any more

of the mob from escaping. The gunman barked an or-der at Curly: "Stay with the prisoner. I'll lead these jaspers!"

Besides Dunbar and Curly, there were now four men left in the lynch mob, three miners and Fred Lar-sen, who owned a mercantile. Dunbar hurriedly tried to organize the men into a fighting force, but they were paying more attention to the small posse which was now at the foot of the hill.

"There ain't been no shots from them trees a spell!" Larsen pointed toward the stream. "We musta hit the owlhoot. Let's take cover there!" Dunbar's loud curses did no good; the four men rode directly at the trees.

A fresh series of gunshots sprayed dirt in front of the panicked riders. The three miners turned their horses toward town but Larsen lost control of his sor-rel and fell, hitting the ground face down. He rolled and sprang to his feet as Reverend Stubby hastily rode by him.

Doc Evans and Clay Adams rode up to the mer-chant, who was examining himself for wounds. "Take it easy, Fred," Evans tried to sound friendly. "The ex-citement is over . . ."

Larsen wasn't listening to the calm words. He looked with raw hatred at the rider who was beside the doctor.

"You weren't too good to take Grady's money! Now you're double crossin' him. You're trash, jus' like that mama o' yours who is always askin' me to let her pay later."

Adams jumped from his horse and smashed a fist into Larsen's mouth. The merchant staggered backwards and Adams had to swing fast to land another hit before Larsen collapsed under the force of the first blow.

"Get up, Larsen!"

Doc Evans slid off his horse, ran to Clay Adams and placed a hand on the young man's chest. "That's enough son, there's no need—"

Adams pushed the doctor away and advanced on Larsen who was struggling to his feet. "You take back what you just said!"

Larsen spit in the young man's direction. Adams began to take another swing at the drunken merchant, but this time two men intervened. Cassius Remick and Doc Evans each grabbed one of Adams' arms and pulled him backward.

"Young fool, you're doin' more harm than—"

Suddenly they heard a shot, followed by a loud scream.

"Stay with the prisoner, I'll lead these jaspers!" Dunbar shouted at Curly, then turned to the four jittery men who composed what was left of the lynch mob.

Curly waved his six-gun at Boyd Matheson. "Don't get no stupid ideas."

Matheson shrugged his shoulders, which felt a bit awkward with his hands tied behind his back. "Looks to me like you gents are the stupid ones. Bull Grady's idea is falling apart. Course, he's back in town sitting all comfortable, while you and Dunbar are ducking bullets. Yeah, looks pretty stupid to me."

Curly moved his gun closer to the prisoner. "You shut your mouth or—"

"Your gang's riding off!" Matheson shouted.

Curly turned his head and Matheson plowed his body against his captor's shoulder and back. Matheson saw Curly fall off the left side of his horse. Boyd slipped his feet from the stirrups and plunged between the two horses. As he hit the ground, Matheson saw the moon reflecting on Curly's six-gun as it tumbled against the dirt. He had to stop his captor from re-claiming that weapon.

Matheson quickly rolled under Curly's horse, then scrambled to his feet as a stunned Curly got up on his knees looking frantically for the gun. Matheson slammed a hard kick against the side of his captor's head. Curly dropped unconscious to the ground, as the sound of hoof beats approached.

Dunbar rode around his partner's limp body, look-ing downward quickly then returning his glance to Matheson. "Think you've made fools of us, don't you?"

"All your pal is going to have is a swelled head. That's nothing compared to what you had planned for me," Matheson said.

Dunbar laughed, pulled his gun from its holster, and aimed at Matheson. "I still got plans, only now they's quicker."

A shot fired. Dunbar screamed as his body lurched

backwards, falling to the ground. Matheson quickly ran to the gun Dunbar had dropped and put his right foot over it. A glance at the fallen gunman revealed that the move wasn't necessary. Dunbar was alive and conscious but convulsing in pain. He wouldn't be threatening anyone for a while.

"Thanks, I'm beholden to you." Matheson spoke as Reverend Stubby holstered his gun and dismounted.

The clergyman pulled a jackknife from his frock coat and began to cut the ropes which bound Matheson's hand. "Yes, you are beholden. But don't worry, I've got plenty of ideas as to how you can repay the favor."

Both of the Mellors came riding toward them laughing. "We followed them fellas fer a spell! Don't worry, that lynch mob won't be comin' back. They're ridin' fast, with their tails tucked 'tween their legs."

Boyd Matheson got a well needed laugh from Hank's remark. It seemed incredible but he knew that at sun up, men who had almost been killers would return to their normal lives, pretending that nothing extraordinary had happened. Matheson noted that Fred Larsen still remained, but he was now riding with Clay Adams, Cassius Remick and the doc. Larsen looked sullen and withdrawn; so did the other three men as they dismounted and joined the group.

The next hour was spent getting what information they could out of Curly. Both Curly and Dunbar were recent additions to Bull Grady's gang. They knew little of the operation. Curly could only confirm that

Grady had instructed them to make sure Matheson ended up dead but not to do the killing themselves unless necessary. They were to prod Fred Larsen and the others into doing the actual hanging.

Curly spoke as he stood near Dunbar, who was being attended to by Doc Evans. The remaining men formed an awkward semi-circle, facing Curly. When Grady's henchman had finished, Reverend Stubby spoke quietly to Fred Larsen.

"You almost committed murder for Bull Grady, Fred. A man who was willing to let you be a killer, while his hands stayed clean."

Larsen's eyes went to the ground. "He wasn't always like that, you know. This is a hard country, Reverend. I had nothing when I got here in sixty-eight. Bull Grady helped me and my family. Not that it cost him anything, but he still helped. He used to be that way."

Reverend Stubby nodded his head. "I know and I understand, Fred. But Bull Grady has changed. He's got to be stopped."

"Reckon so," Larsen said, but he said nothing else. The store owner mounted his horse and rode off.

"Do you think Larsen might join up with us?" Cassius Remick asked.

"Fred won't be opposing us anymore," the clergyman replied. "Right now, I'll settle for that."

Reverend Stubby turned his attention to Doc Evans. "Can Dunbar ride soon?"

"Well, yes, if he takes it easy."

The reverend looked angrily at the two outlaws. "I suggest you two jaspers camp by the stream for the night. At sun up ride far away from here. Bull Grady would kill you for what just happened. To be honest, we're inclined to do the same thing. You're getting a second chance. Don't botch it."

Both Curly and Dunbar mumbled assent.

The pastor gave the other men a sideways grin. "I'm hereby calling a meeting of the town council for tonight, as soon as we get back to town. Matheson and Adams are invited to attend the meeting. That's quite an honor. Congratulations, gents."

"What's this meeting about?" Doc Evans asked.

"Bull Grady will soon know that his usual ways won't work this time around," the pastor explained. "From now on, it's open warfare. In the next few days you gentlemen will need to do a lot of praying. But when you do, keep your eyes open and your guns handy."

Chapter Eight

Once again Boyd Matheson was sitting at a long table. Only this time Clay Adams was sitting on his right. They were inside Remick's general store, surrounded by members of the town council, all of them looking both determined and scared.

Without being too obvious about it, Matheson watched Laurel Remick as she moved around the table pouring cups of coffee. Depending on how the light from the kerosene lamps reflected on it, Laurel's hair appeared blond or red. Matheson had only seen such beautiful hair once before, on Ann . . .

Reverend Stubby called the meeting to order. Laurel eased into a chair beside her father, across from Matheson. She reached downward and gave Perkins a pat on his head.

Matheson tried to ignore the smoke from several

cigarettes and Doc Evans' pipe that was already forming a cloud over the table. But the gunman's chest felt tight and his mind couldn't escape from the past. Several minutes had passed before he began to actually hear the clergyman's words.

". . . Grady failed to kill Boyd Matheson and the whole town will know it by morning. Bull Grady will have to strike again soon. The election is the day after tomorrow and he can't afford to look weak.

"As you gentlemen," Reverend Stubby paused and nodded politely at Laurel, "and Miss Remick, are aware, the town council has the authority to appoint a sheriff and one deputy. I recommend we offer the job of sheriff to Mr. Boyd Matheson and ask Clay Adams to serve as his deputy."

Applause and shouts of approval greeted the recommendation. Matheson felt dizzy. He blinked his eyes several times as the room seemed to be going out of focus.

"Sorry." The gunman stood up and walked out of the store. He stopped on the boardwalk and took in several deep breaths. A short bout of coughing followed.

"Mr. Matheson, are you all right?"

Matheson turned to see Laurel Remick standing behind him. He smiled nervously. "I'm fine, thank you Miss Remick. I just needed some fresh air."

Laurel took a few steps forward and faced him directly. "Mr. Matheson, you owe this town nothing. I wouldn't blame you for riding off right now. But, you are very much needed here. I hope you will at least consider being our sheriff."

"I think Clay Adams might be the man this town needs," Matheson replied. "He can handle a gun."

Laurel lowered her voice slightly. "He can handle a gun but he can't handle himself. Not yet. I heard my grandfather and Doctor Evans talking about what happened tonight. But they seem to think Clay Adams would make a fine deputy if he had someone like you to work with him."

The gunman paused, then spoke slowly. "Wearing a badge is serious business. It's a calling almost, like the reverend has a calling to preach."

Laurel noted the intensity in Matheson's voice and eyes. "Have you been a lawman before?"

"Once," he answered. "Then . . ."

"Something awful happened?"

The gunman nodded his head.

Laurel fidgeted with her hands before speaking. "I'm truly sorry, Mr. Matheson, but if you don't become our sheriff I'm afraid that something awful will happen to this town and to the decent citizens who live in it."

The young woman's voice began to tremble. She said nothing for a moment then spoke in a light, humorous voice. "Besides, maybe you do have a calling to be a lawman. Jonah tried to escape his calling and ended up being swallowed by a fish. I hope you don't end up in the belly of a whale, Mr. Matheson."

Boyd Matheson laughed out loud. "Wouldn't be

surprised. Fish do seem to be a lot smarter than me. I've tried using a fishing pole many times, but nothing much ever comes of it."

There was some more laughter, then Matheson looked into the sky. Laurel didn't speak, sensing that the man beside her was struggling with a flood of ugly memories.

His gaze suddenly returned to earth. "I guess folks are in for a surprise tomorrow."

"What do you mean?"

"Well, tonight they saw a man on trial for murder, tomorrow they're going see that same man wearing a sheriff's badge. Can't blame them for being a bit surprised."

"Thank you Mr. Matheson!" She reached out with both hands and grabbed Matheson's right arm, then hastily let go.

The gunman looked around nervously at nothing in particular. "Guess I better get inside and be sworn in."

The swearing in was quick and not too ceremonious. The entire town council stood while Reverend Stubby had Boyd, and then Clay, raise his right hand and place his left on the Bible while swearing to uphold the law. Matheson watched carefully while Clay Adams took the oath. The young man looked subdued. The gunman figured Adams had received some harsh criticism for going after the shopkeeper. Matheson knew there wasn't much sense in riding over that territory again with the kid. There was a lot more the deputy had to learn, and learn fast.

"Sheriff Matheson and Deputy Adams, I want you to report for your first day of work tomorrow at nine in the morning."

"Why so late, Reverent?" Hank Mellor asked.

"That will allow plenty of time for the town to find out what has happened. There will be lots of eyes watching the sheriff's office at nine," Reverend Stubby answered.

Perkins barked playfully. Laurel scratched his ears. Her face reflected concern, not playfulness. "The mayor appointed Pete Wheeler as acting sheriff—"

"He had that right," Cassius Remick interrupted. "But accordin' to the charter, the town council appoints the permanent sheriff."

Laurel's face lost none of its worry. "But what if Pete Wheeler doesn't see it that way? What if Bull Grady orders him to remain sheriff and has a gang back him up?"

"Those questions will be answered tomorrow morning at nine," Reverend Stubby said. "It may give us an idea of what Grady's war plan is going to be. Whatever the plan, you can be sure of what the goal is— to get rid of each one of us. Permanently."

The pastor paused for a moment as each person in the room contemplated the words he had just spoken. He thought about offering everyone a final chance to resign from the town council and then realized how unnecessary that gesture was. These people were not the kind who quit. Quitters would have left a long time back.

Reverend Stubby led the group in a brief prayer. "May God bless each one of us," he said after the "amen."

Nobody left the store immediately. That didn't surprise the gunfighter. Facing a common threat, people would want to huddle together for mutual strength and encouragement. The new sheriff watched while his deputy ambled over to the Remicks and tried to make conversation. Matheson couldn't hear what they were saying, but it was apparent that Clay's main interest was in getting to know Laurel Remick better. That bothered Matheson a bit and he felt mad at himself because of it.

The gunman told himself there were other things he needed to be thinking about. After a few minutes, he noticed Doc Evans leaving the store and followed after him. Matheson caught up with the doctor just as he was stepping off the boardwalk outside.

"Doc, I've been saying thanks to a lot of folks tonight. Don't want to leave you out."

"No need," Evans replied without slowing his stride. "You've agreed to be sheriff, that's plenty thanks enough."

Matheson continued walking beside the doctor. "You know, when I took a tumble off that horse tonight, well, I think something inside me might have got hurt. Just a little. Think maybe you could open up your bag of tricks and give me what you doctors call an examination?

Doc Evans looked carefully at his companion. This

request had nothing to do with falling off a horse and the doctor knew it, but it wouldn't be the first time he had gone along with a charade. "Why sure, come along to my place. We'll start off with what folks in the east call a night cap. Having the sheriff right there will keep me honest about my drinking."

The two men continued to walk toward the doctor's home. They looked inconspicuous and, that late at night, there was no one to notice them.

Or so they thought.

Laurel Remick crept quietly and quickly through the grassy field toward the house. She could see the shadows of Doctor Evans and Boyd Matheson on the curtains that covered the partially open side window. The young woman knew that window served the part of the house Doctor Evans used for his office.

She stopped and leaned against a small willow tree. Laurel felt both ashamed of herself and a bit giddy at the same time. It had been at least five years since she had tried to sneak up and spy on anyone and, well, it was a lot of fun.

But she was nineteen years old now, grown-up. She needed to act like an adult. Laurel occasionally found herself confused as to how grownups should conduct themselves, but she was certain that sneaking up on someone's house and listening in to private conversations would not be regarded as adult behavior.

Still, Laurel felt compelled to do it. Boyd Matheson's coughing spell outside of the store had worried her. Then she had watched him approach Doctor Evans in that casual way men have when they are trying to disguise more serious motives.

The young woman peeked around the trunk of the tree. She was too far away to hear what the two men were saying. A hedge ran around Doctor Evans' house and was only a few feet from the window. Laurel bent down low and began a fast dash toward the hedge.

The woman had only ran a few steps when she heard a rustling sound moving at her from behind. She turned and saw Perkins running toward her joyfully. When the dog's eyes met hers he began to bark. Laurel continued to dash for the hedge, but dropped to the ground when a hand appeared on one of the curtains.

". . . sounds like that fool dog, Perkins," she could hear Doc Evans saying.

Boyd Matheson's voice came in. "Yeah. He does have a bark more high pitched then most mongrels. Does he play around here much?"

"No, that's the strange thing," Evans replied. "He usually sticks pretty close to Laurel Remick . . ."

As if to prove the doctor's point, Perkins was now licking Laurel's face as she remained pinned to the ground. The dog had been snoring away when Laurel left the store to spy on the doctor and Matheson.

"Guess you weren't sleeping as hard as I thought," she whispered to the dog as she scratched his ears, trying to prevent any more barking.

Laurel was close enough to the hedge to be shielded from Doc Evans' eyes but the moment the two men moved away from the window she could no longer hear what they were saying. She needed to move closer. The young woman crawled stealthily toward the house until she was directly in front of the hedge. Perkins moved with her, panting but not barking.

Laurel could now make out the words the two men were saying. Boyd Matheson's voice was heavy with a forced cheerfulness. "That stuff surely does taste awful, Doc."

Doc Evans' laugh was equally as artificial. "Don't believe I've ever given a patient anything that did taste good. I'm not running a restaurant here."

"So, I have to take my medicine like a good boy and give up smokes," Matheson said, trying to keep his voice light.

Doc Evans was a bit more serious. "I think you knew cigarettes were hurting you. You sure noticed the coughing fits they gave you."

There was an awkward pause. Laurel had a feeling of trepidation. She wasn't enjoying this anymore. Matheson's voice became a monotone. "So if I take the medicine and stay away from tobacco, how much time will I have?"

Evans sighed deeply before speaking. "A doctor gets asked a lot of questions he can't answer. I would guess two, maybe three years. If you keep on smoking cigarettes, you'll have less time, I can tell you that for sure. I wish there was more I could say."

That forced cheerfulness returned to Matheson's

voice. "You told me what I need to know and you told me straight. A man can't ask for more."

The voices coming out the window receded as the two men left the office area and ambled toward the front door of the house. Laurel could no longer hear anything but she didn't leave. For over a half hour she remained on the ground where Perkins gently licked the moisture from her face as her body convulsed in a silent and anguished cry.

Chapter Nine

Boyd Matheson walked slowly toward the hotel. A cool night breeze brushed against him and he laughed at his own astonishment over the pleasant weather. "When a man learns he's dying there should be thunder, lighting and such all over the skies," he whispered to himself. He wondered what the weather had been like in Washington on the night Abraham Lincoln was assassinated. Probably nothing special, he decided.

Matheson kicked a stone in front of him and watched it land several feet away and to his right. He'd seen lots of men die, the gunfighter mused, so what was so special about his own death?

As he stepped onto the boardwalk in front of the hotel, Boyd Matheson stopped and looked around at the town which now appeared peaceful and tranquil. In less than a day, there would be serious bloodshed in Gradyville; men would die. He was sure of that. But what would be the outcome of all the killing? Would Gradyville be a better place? Would Laurel Remick and the rest of the good people in the town have a decent place to live and raise kids?

The gunfighter walked into the hotel and headed directly to his room. After entering, he locked the door and propped a chair under the doorknob. He grabbed the bottle of medicine out of his hip pocket and ripped off the label so that no one who happened to see the bottle would know its purpose. He placed the medicine in the top drawer of the room's chest of drawers. The bed creaked as he sat on it and took off his boots. As he lay across the bed, his clothes still on, Matheson knew that sleep was far away despite his weariness.

He desperately wanted a cigarette. And why shouldn't he smoke? If he only had a little time left he might as well enjoy a few pleasures.

Matheson whirled off the bed and stepped toward the chest of drawers and the saddle bags that were lying on top of it. He opened one of the bags, retrieving a pouch of tobacco and a pack of papers. For a moment he stood absolutely still, staring at the items in his hand.

The gunman bolted toward the room's only window. He flung it open and tossed the tobacco and papers outside. Then he closed the window, watching as the tobacco pouch and the papers hit the ground. A cat crept from out of an alley beside the hotel and approached the items cautiously.

"I'd stay away from that stuff if I was you," Matheson said quietly, "or else you'll use up those nine lives real quick."

Matheson began to pace around the small room. He had a job to do and he had to stay far away from anything that might stop him from doing that job.

And for the first time in many years he had a job he really wanted to do. The gunman gave a short, bitter laugh. For the first time in a long while Matheson felt like he had a reason to live. He wanted to defeat Bull Grady. He wanted to make Gradyville a safe and good town, a town where . . .

He returned to the bed and his thoughts returned to Laurel Remick. He tried to banish her from his mind. Laurel Remick was a very fine and beautiful young woman. She didn't need a dying man thinking about her.

But she looked so much like Ann. Gradyville reminded him so much of Stanton, Texas. His arrival in Gradyville—could it really have been at noon the previous day—started much like his first day in Stanton. Matheson laughed again, only this time there was nothing bitter about it. Yep, that first day in Stanton, Texas had really been something.

Matheson was twenty years old when he rode into Stanton looking for work. Jobs were hard to find in those years immediately after the war, but the young man had heard things were a bit different around Stanton. A local rancher, Isaac Montoya, was doing better than most and always had need for extra hands.

Matheson had just reached the edge of town when he heard a woman scream. He halted his horse as a yellow haired angel ran in front of him. Two men were running after her. They tailed her up the steps and onto the large porch of a two-story house. The young woman placed herself in front of the door, blocking the entrance.

"Aren't ya gonna ask us in, sweet thang?" The heavyset man took a swig from a whiskey bottle and placed it on the banister that fronted the porch.

"I want you both to leave," the woman declared emphatically. "This is a boarding house—"

The other man, a short scrawny creature, interrupted. "So, let us come in an' get ourselves boarded—"

"Excuse me, gents!" All three people on the porch turned toward the stranger on horseback, noticing him for the first time.

"I think you men should move on and allow the lady to get on with her business."

The heavyset man snorted and smirked. "Listen up, stranger. Ike, me, and a lot of other cowhands have been workin' like dogs for months. Now, we're gonna have us some fun."

"I reckon this town is like most." Matheson said casually.

"Whaddya mean?" Ike shot back.

"There are lots of places where a man can have a good time," Matheson explained. "But this ain't one of them. Move on."

The heavyset man leered at the woman, then looked back at Matheson. "I can have me a good time right here."

The rider patted the neck of his horse, pretending not to have heard the last remark. "I hear tell that in a house owned by respectable folks, a bottle of whiskey can't even stand up. Before long, it'll explode."

Ike gave the stranger a lopsided grin. "How's that?"

With a smooth, fast motion Matheson drew his gun and fired at the whiskey bottle on the banister. The bottle shattered instantly. The bullet cut a harmless path to the side of the house.

"Yep. Put a bottle of whiskey where it don't belong and that'll happen every time." Matheson smiled politely as he returned his gun to its holster.

Ike stood flabbergasted. "Tom, I think maybe the gent's got hisself a point. Maybe we should mosey ourselves down to the Lady Luck Saloon. Won't nothin' blow up there."

"Yeah, maybe so." Tom looked with admiration and curiosity at the newcomer. "Where'd ya learn to shoot like that, friend?"

"I was in the army for a while."

Tom smiled and shrugged his shoulders. "So was I. Army taught me to shoot some, mostly taught me to drink. Guess I'll start workin' again on that right now." He turned to the young woman. "Sorry fer causin' ya trouble. Ike and me just got a little outta hand."

The woman smiled pleasantly. "There was no harm done."

As the two men left the porch and headed for the saloon, Matheson dismounted and using a few rocks, hastily tethered his horse to the ground. He noticed that the yellow-haired angel was carrying a bag full of something; he wanted to talk with her before she took the items into the house. He almost ran up the porch stairs while taking off his hat. When he made it onto the porch he became nervous and completely still, unable to think of a thing to say.

The young lady helped him out. "Thank you for helping, Mister . . ."

"Matheson, Boyd Matheson."

"Mr. Matheson, my name is Ann Farley."

"Pleased to meet you, Miss Farley."

Once again, Matheson could think of nothing to say and, once again, he didn't have to think about it very long. The front door of the house banged open and Boyd was staring into the barrel of a shotgun.

"Git on that horse of yours an' ride, or they'll be pickin' up your teeth on the other end of town!"

Ann looked embarrassed. She smiled weakly at Matheson, then spoke to the elderly lady holding the shotgun. "Aunt Clara, please . . ."

"Got outta bed just in time to see this varmint shootin' at the house. Came down quick as I could."

"Aunt Clara, this is Boyd Matheson. He was running off two of Montoya's cowhands. They started giving me trouble on my way back from the store." Ann Farley's face was completely red when she spoke again to Matheson. "Aunt Clara and I run this boarding house."

Matheson nodded at the elderly lady. "I'm pleased to meet you, Ma'am."

Ann placed a hand on the barrel of the shotgun and gently pushed it lower so it wasn't pointing at the newcomer. "Mr. Matheson just rode in," she said to her aunt. "And he stopped to help me."

Aunt Clara stepped out onto the porch, the door slamming shut behind her. She looked over the stranger. "Well, he sure ain't one of Isaac Montoya's boys. Them fellers bathe before they come inta town!"

The young woman's eyes darted to the floor. Boyd Matheson suddenly became very aware of the fact that he was standing on a partially enclosed porch and there was no wind blowing. "You got a good point, Ma'am. I need to be finding a hotel and getting cleaned up a bit. It's been nice meeting both of you ladies."

Matheson scrambled off the porch. Ann Farley hastily set her shopping bag on the banister and caught up to the newcomer as he reached his horse. "Mr. Matheson, please forgive my aunt, it's just that, well, she's eccentric."

Boyd felt encouraged. He was happy Ann didn't share her aunt's low opinion of him. "I hope she's getting proper care for her, ah, *eccenthric.*"

Ann Farley looked a bit confused and Matheson suspected he had not said exactly the right thing. The young woman hastily changed the subject. "The Farley House serves dinner every evening at six. Please pleasure us with your company tonight."

"Thank you, Miss Farley, I'd be pleased to do that." Matheson glanced at Aunt Clara. Her eyes were filled with suspicion, but at least she wasn't pointing a gun at him.

After mounting up and delivering a few awkward good-byes, Matheson rode down Main Street into the heart of Stanton. There was a festive mood in the town, as guns occasionally fired and loud voices shrieked from the Lady Luck Saloon. Boyd took his horse to the livery stable, then walked back toward the Crawford Hotel which was located next to the saloon. Matheson had been serious about that room and bath.

"Hey, stranger!" A slim man of about forty was beckoning to him from the door of a grocery store directly across the street from the saloon. The man extended his right hand as Matheson approached him.

"Fred Burns is the name," the man said nervously as he shook hands with the newcomer. "You must be the gent what did that fancy shooting in front of Farley's Boarding House."

"Word travels fast," Matheson said.

"Stanton's a small town," Burns explained. "Word ain't got all that far to travel."

Across the street the sounds of a fight could be heard coming from the saloon. Two men slammed against the swinging doors of the Lady Luck and went sprawling onto the boardwalk outside. Several men followed them out of the saloon and began to cheer as the two men continued to fight. It was obvious that the spectators had placed a wager on the outcome of the brawl.

"Isaac Montoya works his boys hard," Burns said. "Course, these are hard times and the men are happy to be working. But mostly Isaac only lets two or three come into town at a time. The rest gotta stay at the ranch."

Both of the fighters and the mob were now in the middle of the street. The combatants were staggering and the crowd cheered louder as the end of the battle was drawing near.

"But I hear Montoya lets all his men come into town together three or four times a year," Matheson said.

Burns nodded his head. "They really do some hoor-awing. This started about two hours ago."

Both fighters had now collapsed. An argument was spreading across the crowd as to which man had dropped first.

"Shouldn't the sheriff be here?" Matheson asked.

"The sheriff of Stanton resigned."

"When?"

"About two hours ago," Burns answered.

"Oh."

"Hope they don't burn me down again," the shop-keeper said.

"Again?"

The shopkeeper pointed to the sign across the front of his store, *Burns' Grocery and Supplies* " 'Burn down Burns', Montoya's men think that's a real knee slapper. You'd think they'd get tired of the joke after a while, but no, they always try to set fire to the place. Isaac pays me back when there's serious damage, still, I'd just as soon not have the trouble."

The noise from the mob was getting louder; Matheson had to raise his voice. "I can understand that! Say, is Mr. Montoya anywhere around?"

"Ain't seen him. Sometimes he rides in with the boys. Sometimes not."

Boyd noticed several men in the crowd pointing at the two fighters lying unconscious on the ground. The argument seemed to be intensifying as to which man had won the fight. No one seemed to be interested in reviving the fighters or helping them to their feet.

"I was hoping to talk to Mr. Montoya about a job."

Fred Burns shook his head. "Afraid you'd be wasting your time."

Boyd cringed. "I'd heard Montoya is doing good."

"He is," the grocer replied. "But not many others are. So, his cowhands just stay put. They don't drift off like they usta, ain't got nowhere to drift to."

Fred Burns looked nervously at the crowd. The voices were becoming angrier. A series of brawls could erupt over who had won the first brawl. He swung his glance back to the young man. "Montoya can't give you no work, but I can. How'd you like to be the sheriff of Stanton, Texas!"

"Well . . ."

"I'm the mayor of this town and can give you the job right now!"

The mayor proceeded to spell out the details of the sheriff's salary. It wasn't much, but it was the first offer of steady pay Boyd Matheson had heard since the war. He took the job much to the elation of Mayor Fred Burns.

"Here's your badge!" Burns reached into his shirt pocket and pulled out a piece of tin. "The last sheriff gave it to me just before he rode off. Ain't much, I know, but if you look at it careful it does sorta look like a star. If you keep the job a while, I'll get another one made up."

"Where's the sheriff's office?"

"Just a few doors up from the Lady Luck. Ain't locked, you'll find all the keys in the desk drawer. Otherwise, ain't much to it, no guns or nothing. You'll have to use your own."

A gunshot sounded behind them. An angry cow-hand, made angrier by alcohol and hot sun, fired a second shot into the air. "I say the money is mine and if I don't get it soon, somebody is gonna die."

The cowhand's threat was met by mocking laughter and coarse shouts. The new sheriff realized the situation was close to a riot. He stepped off the boardwalk and approached the crowd. The men gradually became quiet. There was a new player in the game, a green-horn sheriff.

Matheson stopped near the middle of the street,

standing a few feet from the cowhand who still held a gun in his right hand. The other men backed away.

"There's no law in this town says a man can't have a good time," Matheson spoke in a loud but calm monotone. "But that don't include firing a gun." The young lawman nodded at the pistol the cowhand was now pointing directly at him. "Put that back in the holster. Now. And make sure it stays there."

The cowhand forced a laugh; the smile on his face was quivering. "You think you can drop me before I pull this trigger."

"I know he can!" Ike scuttled out of the crowd to the cowhand's side. "He's the one Tom and me was jawin' 'bout. He's good, Ben, put your gun away."

Ben's smile vanished, replaced by fear and confusion. The gun remained in his hand and began to shake. The cowhand needed a face-saving way out.

Matheson gave it to him. "Forget the gun, Ben. After all, you may have a free drink coming."

"Free drink?"

Matheson nodded at the two fighters, who were now on their feet watching the new sheriff along with the rest of Montoya's men. "One of those gents won a lot of money for some folks. Seems to me the least the winners can do is buy drinks for the jaspers who lost. After all, it was a pretty close fight."

Nervous but good-natured chortles skidded across the crowd. Ben laughed, shrugged his shoulders and holstered the gun.

Ike and Tom had spread the word about the new

sheriff's speed with a gun. Not a bad start, but Matheson knew more was needed. "Before you fellas go back inside, I need to honor a tradition in this town."

"Tradition?" Ike shouted.

"Yeah." Matheson's voice became casual and friendly. "The new Sheriff of Stanton always puts on a shooting demonstration for the citizens of the town."

Ike scratched his head. "Who started that tradition?"

"I did," Matheson said.

For the next twenty minutes or so, the new sheriff put bullets through an array of tin cans and old whiskey bottles with his six-shooter. He saved his biggest surprise for the end of the show, when the most people had collected in front of the Lady Luck Saloon. As the crowd gasped and then applauded, the lawman had to smile inwardly. Strange, the things that impress people.

"Show's over," Matheson holstered his gun. "Sure been nice seeing all you folks. Looking forward to meeting every one of you. But right now, I best get to work!"

There were friendly laughs and a few shouts of "welcome" as the crowd dispersed. Matheson's first stop was Burns' Grocery and Supplies, where the mayor drew him a map of the town. The new sheriff used the map to do his first round.

Montoya's men kept the sheriff busy breaking up fights and preventing drunken cowhands from doing any serious damage. The sun had been down for almost two hours before Matheson got to inspect his office.

Fred Burns had said there wasn't much in the office and he was right; a scarred desk and two chairs comprised the room's only furniture. Matheson walked across the office and opened the door that led to the jail cells. To his surprise there were three large cells that didn't appear at all rickety.

"I guess they need them," the lawman said to himself. As he stepped back into the office, he began to realize that hours had passed since he last had anything to eat. Fred Burns had said something about free meals being part of the sheriff's pay, but hadn't given any details. No doubt the mayor was still in his store, in case anyone tried to burn down Burns. Matheson needed to drop by there again and find out where he could get the free grub.

As the lawman stepped onto the boardwalk outside his office he almost collided with Ann Farley. The young woman was carrying a supper tray and the silverware jangled as she abruptly stopped.

"Sorry—" They spoke the same word in unison, then both laughed self consciously.

"Amanda Burns came by the Farley House earlier and told us her husband had appointed you as sheriff," Ann explained. "When you didn't show up for dinner, I figured you were too busy, so I brought this here."

"That's very nice of you." Matheson took off his hat, opened the door to the office and motioned for the young woman to enter.

"It's really my duty," Ann's voice became jittery as

she carried the tray to the battered desk and placed it there. "You see, the Farley Boarding House has an arrangement with the town to provide three meals a day to the sheriff. The sheriff can eat at the Farley or we bring his meal here to him. Sheriff Dexter did it both ways at different times, till he ran off today." She suddenly lifted her voice. "Now, he ran off 'cause Montoya's men scared him, not 'cause of the food!"

"Oh, I'm sure that's right!" Matheson looked down at the tray, then looked up at the young woman, who was now standing in front of him with her hands folded.

"Well then . . ." Ann looked toward the front door as if getting ready to leave.

"Miss Farley, I've been spending most of the day handling a bunch of crazy-headed cowhands and I've got a lot more of that work ahead of me tonight." Matheson nervously gazed about the office, swallowed, then continued. "You would be doing me a favor to stay and talk a spell while I eat my dinner. That is, if you're a mind to."

"Why, thank you Mr. Matheson, I believe I would enjoy that."

Matheson hastily brushed the dust from one of the chairs with his hat. Ann Farley nodded a thank you as she sat down. The new sheriff sat behind his desk but leaned away from his guest, remembering that he hadn't yet taken a bath.

The next several minutes were filled with stilted conversation as Boyd Matheson complimented his food and Ann Farley assured the new sheriff that Stanton, Texas was a wonderful place to live.

"Is your aunt the only kin you've got in this town?" Matheson asked.

"Aunt Clara is the only kin I've got anywhere," Ann replied. "Mother died when I was a little girl, and I lost my father when I was twelve. Both of my brothers died in the war. I heard you say that you were in the army, Mr. Matheson."

The sheriff pushed some food around with his fork. "I served in the Union Army. That won't make me too popular around here."

Ann Farley fidgeted with her hands for a moment, then spoke in a determined manner. "I'm sure you believed strongly in the Union cause."

"No, I didn't." Matheson laid his fork down and looked directly at the young woman. "Like you, I lost my ma when I was young. Pa and me couldn't seem to agree on anything. Must have been my fault. My brother and two sisters got along with Pa okay. I couldn't seem to get along with anyone."

Matheson's gaze remained fixed on the young woman. "Then the war broke out. The army was someplace for me to go. I lied about my age and joined up when I was fifteen. Guess I would have gone almost anywhere to get away from that farm in Ohio and my Pa."

"I can understand that, Mr. Matheson."

"That's kind of you to say, Miss Farley, but a man shouldn't go to killing other men just because he's got nothing else to do. And that's what I did. I'm not proud of it."

Boyd Matheson suddenly felt embarrassed. He couldn't understand why he had revealed so much of himself to this young woman whom he barely knew.

"I've cried a lot because of the war." Ann pressed her lips together. Matheson was afraid that she would start crying again, but when she spoke her voice was firm. "The hurt will always be there, of course, but we must leave such things in the past. I'm trying to do that. You must also try, Mr. Matheson."

The couple stared intently at each other, then a feeling of nervousness overcame them both. Ann Farley realized that the direction of their conversation needed to be changed.

"And while we're talking on such serious matters, Sheriff, you've got an important decision to make!" The young woman's voice was playful.

Matheson was grateful for the sudden change in mood. "Now, what might that be?"

"Why, the new sheriff of Stanton, Texas needs a place to live, and I know where that is!" Ann slapped the desk, then continued. "There's a vacant room at the Farley Boarding House. Our prices are lower than the Crawford Hotel and the service is better!"

Boyd Matheson laughed quietly to himself as he stared at the blank wall in the Gradyville Hotel. He had moved into the Farley Boarding House that night and started the happiest year of his life. He reckoned that he and Ann knew they were in love with each other from the start, but they had to be cautious. They were living under the same roof and Matheson didn't want to do anything that would sully Ann's reputation.

They became man and wife a little less than four months later. During that time, Matheson was able to persuade Aunt Clara that he was the right man for her niece. "I ain't gonna be here much longer," Clara told him the night before the wedding. "But that don't worry me none. I know you'll take good care of Ann."

Aunt Clara died six weeks after the wedding and Ann took over all the responsibilities of running the Farley Boarding House. The couple had decided that Boyd should remain the sheriff of Stanton for a couple more years. They would save their money and use it to expand the Farley into a fine hotel which would be renamed *The Matheson*. Then Boyd Matheson would resign as sheriff and he and Ann would run the hotel together.

Matheson closed his eyes and pressed his lips together. After more than ten years, Aunt Clara's words still twisted inside him, "I know you'll take good care of Ann."

"Time for the sheriff to have some grub!" Ann smiled at her husband as she bustled into the office carrying a now familiar tray.

"I'm going to need every bite of it," Matheson

laughed as he stood up from his desk. "Montoya's men are coming to town for a few days of hoorawing. I'll have to sleep in the office tonight."

"That surely is bad news," Ann set the tray on the desk, then looked directly at her husband. The couple shared an intimate smile. "But don't worry," the young woman continued, "I'll keep things in order at the house."

Matheson trailed his wife as she headed for the door. "Now, I don't want you doing too much . . ."

Ann laughed softly, turned and bounced an index finger on her husband's nose. "You know what the doctor said, I won't have to start taking it easy for a few months yet."

"Yeah, but—"

"Hush! It is not proper for a tough lawman to be clucking like a mother hen."

The couple brushed their lips together in a quick, sensuous kiss, then Matheson opened the door, stood on the boardwalk and watched as his wife walked back toward the Farley Boarding House.

Gunshots and loud shrieks burst out as three riders galloped into town, firing their guns. The first wave of Isaac Montoya's men were arriving. Ann looked back and smiled at her husband who shrugged his shoulders in an exaggerated, comical manner.

It took no more than a moment. One cowhand tried to fire his gun into the air but he didn't have control of his horse or his aim. The bullet glanced off the stone wall of a stage depot and this new trajectory led it straight towards Ann.

"Ann!" Boyd Matheson continued to shout his wife's name as he ran toward her body. From a corner of his eye he could see the face of the cowhand who had fired the deadly bullet. The man was laughing, unaware of the destruction he had wrought. But one of his companions was looking back with terrified eyes.

"Ann!" Matheson crouched over his wife's body and knew immediately that she was gone. A horrible coldness fell over him. He gripped Ann's hand and began to stroke her arm slowly, as he had done many times before when comforting her.

He continued to hold onto his wife's hand as her body was carried to the large shed behind the doctor's house. Over the last year, Matheson had sent a few men to that shed. Men who were killers and thieves. Leaving Ann in this place seemed to be an unspeakable blasphemy.

Several arms pulled Matheson out of the shed. As he fought to go back inside, one of the many words pelting him suddenly penetrated his consciousness. "Sheriff . . ."

The word sounded strange, assigning an identity to him that he no longer felt. No longer wanted. But, yes, he was the sheriff of Stanton, Texas and a sheriff had a duty to arrest killers.

Matheson broke loose from the crowd around him

and walked toward the Lady Luck Saloon. The laughing face of his wife's murderer remained singed in his mind. Matheson knew that the man he needed to kill would be holed up in the saloon surrounded by Isaac Montoya's other hands. The sheriff didn't care.

As Boyd Matheson approached the saloon, he noted that the place was crowded but anxiously silent, waiting for the sheriff and the violence he would bring.

Matheson stepped through the saloon's swinging doors and was greeted by Isaac Montoya. The ranch owner rose from a table where he had been sitting and removed his hat. Montoya was a short, muscular man. There was a softness in his eyes that Boyd had never seen before.

"I'm sorry about yer wife, Sheriff." The rancher spoke in a quiet voice but he could be easily heard.

"Thank you, Mr. Montoya." Matheson's eyes did a quick scan and stopped on the young man at the far end of the bar. Two of Montoya's strongest men surrounded the kid.

"He's a killer." Boyd nodded toward the kid while shifting his eyes back to the rancher. "I'm arresting him."

The softness vanished from Montoya's expression, replaced by fire. "I can't let you do that, Sheriff. It bein' an accident—"

"That doesn't change the fact that a woman is dead!" Matheson shouted.

"If he'd done it on purpose, I'd a brought him to you myself!" Montoya slammed a fist onto the table in front of him. "But Jimmy's just a fool kid, I can't let you jail him."

The boss' "fool kid" remark humiliated Jimmy. He had to show he was a man. Jimmy took a few steps away from the bar. "Don't let losing one woman worry ya none, Sheriff. I'm sure there are plenty o' gals right here in the Lady Luck that'd be happy to oblige you."

Isaac Montoya cringed and looked away from the sheriff. Matheson marched toward the kid. He didn't notice the wave of Montoya's hand.

Jimmy panicked as his protectors moved away from him. He would have to face the advancing lawman on his own. The boy took a step backward and stumbled but managed to stay on his feet.

"I ain't scared of ya!" The words came out as a frantic cry. Jimmy barely had his gun out of his holster when Matheson slapped it out of his hand and landed a vicious torrent of punches on the boy's head.

Jimmy's body seemed to bounce between the bar and his attacker. The boy was barely conscious when he scrambled on top of the bar in a pathetic attempt to escape. He flopped onto the floor behind the bar, flailing his arms like a wounded animal as he tried to get up.

The bartender backed away as Matheson jumped over the bar and drew his gun. A jumbled string of slurred words came from Jimmy's bleeding mouth.

Montoya ran toward the lawman. "No, Sheriff, no, the kid's just sixteen—"

Boyd Matheson bent down and fired his gun. A horrible shriek filled the saloon.

Isaac Montoya's body slouched. The rancher closed his eyes for a moment, then slowly made his way around to the back of the bar. Montoya and the sheriff remained silent as they passed by each other. The grim expression on the rancher's face soon gave way to a look of wonderment, then a chagrinned smile as he looked down at the young man sprawled on the floor.

"Stop yer cryin'!" Montoya yelled at Jimmy as he motioned for several men to help him. "The sheriff done you a favor. He shot off yer trigger finger. You can still punch cows and scratch dirt. But forget any notions about bein' a gunfighter. Good thing!"

Montoya laughed as he ordered his men to get Jimmy to the doctor. His face suddenly turned serious. "Sheriff!"

Boyd Matheson stopped at the swinging doors and turned to face the rancher. The soft expression returned to Montoya's face. "You done a fine thing. You coulda killed the boy. He drawed on you. A lesser man would of."

Matheson said nothing.

Isaac's eyes shifted down for a moment, then he continued. "I don't like sayin' this, Sheriff, but leave town. It ain't right, but there's nothin' here for you but hurt. Go a long way from here and start new."

Boyd Matheson turned and left the saloon.

The rancher's advice was repeated, in cautious whispers, to Matheson many times over the next few weeks. Matheson noticed that people were no longer comfortable around him. And it wasn't because of Ann's death; folks in Stanton, Texas had plenty of experience in dealing with tragedy. It was because Boyd Matheson had become a different man: a cold, empty man who seemed to walk through each day like a sullen child performing a chore he hated.

For a while, the sheriff did what was required of him. He attended his wife's funeral, turned over the Farley House to a young couple he and Ann had been friends with, and trained a new deputy. Exactly six weeks after that bullet ricocheted into Ann's forehead, Matheson handed the sheriff's badge to his deputy and wished him luck. "I won't be back," he said, leaving the office. Boyd Matheson rode out of town at sunup the next day.

Matheson couldn't remember the name of the next town he landed in, or the name of the man whose wife had been shot down because she walked into a bank with two nervous robbers inside. He did remember the man's bitterness because an elderly lawman and a posse of merchants couldn't catch up with the killers. Matheson accepted the man's offer and brought the two crooks back. One was alive, the other Matheson had been forced to kill. Matheson explained what happened to the town sheriff, who wasn't inclined to ask many questions.

The prisoner who came back alive claimed that he had nothing to do with killing the woman, but everyone said that the snake was guilty and would hang. Boyd Matheson didn't care. He collected his pay and left town before the trial.

* * *

Matheson slapped the tear that was traveling toward his jaw. He noticed that the darkness outside was beginning to surrender ground. His first day as sheriff of Gradyville would begin in only a few hours. He needed to be ready.

The gunfighter closed his eyes. "Got some things to do before I die," he mumbled to himself before sleep finally found him.

Chapter Ten

Boyd Matheson casually sipped his second cup of coffee as he smiled and nodded at the elderly couple who were strolling by the restaurant. Returning his cup to the saucer he spoke to his dining companion.

"It's important to remember that a lawman needs to be something of a politician. In a lot of towns they elect the sheriff. They might do that here some day. Can't expect folks to vote for you if you don't smile at them now and again."

Clay Adams frowned, picked up his fork and, noticing he had already eaten all of his breakfast, put it down again. "Is that why you made a fuss about havin' a table in front of the window, so you could do your politickin'?"

"Drink your coffee. They serve good java here."

Matheson nodded at Clay's cup, then looked back out the window. "I'm a man of many talents."

"Is that so!" Adams drank his coffee but it didn't improve his edgy temperament.

"That's so!" Boyd Matheson replied cheerfully. "Lawman, politician and showman. A good showman knows that the bigger the crowd, the better."

"Is that why we're waitin' 'till nine before we start for the sheriff's office?" A note of respect crept into Adams' voice. "You and the reverend want everyone in town to know there's a new sheriff—"

"And a new deputy." Matheson waved cordially at two young boys who were peering in the window as they sauntered by. "You'll notice that folks all seem to be walking in the same direction, toward the sheriff's office. Yep. We're going to have us a pretty good crowd."

Three shots sounded followed by cheering and applause. This time, Clay Adams looked intently out the window. "What in—"

"I was expecting this," Matheson took another sip of coffee. "Pete Wheeler has decided to put on a show too. Guess it's about time to find out who the best showman is."

Both men rose from the table slowly. Boyd Matheson complimented the couple who owned the restaurant on their fine food, paid for both meals, then strolled out of the restaurant with Clay Adams behind him.

There were more shots and more cheering as Matheson and Adams walked toward the sheriff's office. Matheson hoped his tension didn't show. His eyes glanced quickly sideways.

The young man walking beside him was a problem, or might be. Matheson didn't know how far he could trust or depend on Clay Adams.

As the two men approached the sheriff's office, Pete Wheeler was in the middle of the street firing at a row of tin cans. A crowd lined both sides of the boardwalk. Cheers again rose up as Wheeler finished a demonstration and began to reload.

"This time, I wantcha to line up five of 'em!" Wheeler shouted. "I'll hit each one of 'em without havin' to reload."

Five tins cans were placed in the road about fifteen feet from Pete Wheeler. As he holstered his gun, Wheeler turned his head slightly and saw the two men approaching but ignored them.

"Ain't a man in the territory can shoot this good!" Wheeler shouted as he prepared to draw.

"I've seen better, Pete!" Boyd Matheson shouted. "You're not bad but I've seen lots better!"

Wheeler's face flashed anger but he said nothing. He drew his gun and fired too quickly. The bullet plowed ground and didn't reach the cans.

"Firing a gun takes skill, Pete." Matheson shoved Wheeler toward the boardwalk. "It don't come easy like pushing around an old man and his granddaughter and busting up their store. Let me show you how it's done."

Matheson drew and fired sending three cans on a fast twirl. He tossed the pistol into his left hand and eliminated the remaining cans with two quick shots.

A stunned silence came from the crowd followed by loud cheers and applause. Strange the things that impress folks, Matheson thought once again as he holstered his gun. That same trick had worked on his first day as the sheriff of Stanton, Texas, so many years ago.

Matheson touched his hat and nodded in appreciation to the crowd. "I want to thank you all for coming out this morning to welcome me and my deputy. Be sure and vote tomorrow. From what everyone says, George Stuart was a fine sheriff and a fine man. He wanted this town to have a fair and honest contest for mayor. I think it is the duty of every one of us to make sure that happens."

Matheson pointed at Clay Adams. "My deputy here thinks it's time for me to shut my mouth and get to work. Guess he's right."

The new sheriff took a few steps toward Pete Wheeler and spoke in a mockingly friendly voice. "I want to thank you for keeping that star nice and shiny for me, Pete." Boyd Matheson ripped the badge from Wheeler's shirt and placed it on his own. "You can go back to doing odd jobs for Bull Grady now."

Matheson was expecting Wheeler to throw a punch. He was surprised by what happened next. Pete Wheeler gazed into the sheriff's office for a moment, then hastily walked away.

Sounds of light laughter came from the crowd as they began to disperse. The new sheriff continued to smile at the citizens as they went on their way, but his mood was cautious.

"We've got company waiting for us in the office," Matheson whispered to his deputy as he reloaded.

Both lawmen had their guns drawn as they entered the office. They were greeted by a deep, threatening laugh.

"Some lawdogs you gents are, afraid of an unarmed businessman." Bull Grady pushed off from the far wall of the office that he had been leaning against. "Pretty good shooting, Sheriff. You can use your left hand as good as your right. There's a fancy name for that—"

"Ambidextrous." Matheson holstered his gun.

"Yeah, that's right." Grady took a puff on his cigar and looked at Clay Adams. "Of course, fancy words don't buy much at the store, do they, boy?"

Grady took a few steps toward the young man, his voice almost fatherly. "That's the way some folks are, they give you a small piece of tin and expect you to risk your life. Not me."

Grady waved his cigar in the direction of the hotel. "Take that hotel of mine, there's always an empty room or two in it. So, I've been thinking, it might be a good idea to let your ma move in there. No charge. Just something extra you get for working for me. Your ma could have a comfortable room and live like a lady. I wantcha to give that some thought."

A haze of cigar smoke now filled the small office.

Clay Adams looked down at the floor and then looked up, waving away the smoke with one hand. "No thank you, Mr. Grady. My ma lives like a lady now. A right smart lady. She knows what kind you are. She cried when I went to work for you. She and my pa taught me right. Guess it's about time I start livin' that way."

"Fool!" The word roared with hate. Grady stomped across the office, then looked back as he reached the door. "I'll try to see to it that they bury you gents with your badges." Grady's voice was lower but the hate was still there. "Of course, that town council will probably want to save the tin, so they won't have to make new stars for the next fools they find." Grady slammed the door as he left.

"There's no turnin' back now." Adams seemed to be talking to himself as much as to his companion. He walked over to the desk, picked up the deputy's badge and pinned it on. "I'm glad," he said.

This time Matheson felt confident as he walked through Gradyville with his deputy beside him. He still didn't know exactly what Clay Adams was capable of, but he did know for certain which side the young man was on.

"You handled yourself real well back there in the office a few minutes ago," Matheson said.

"I ain't so sure. I made Grady even madder than he was before. 'Course, he was already plannin' to kill us all. Guess there ain't much more worse he can do."

Matheson looked around the town. "After this, we'll

do our rounds separately. I thought it would be good if, right off, everyone saw the new sheriff and deputy on the job."

Adams smirked. "You sure are good at this politickin'. When do you suppose this town will start electin' the sheriff?"

"Right now, Let's just worry about the election for mayor."

The quiet was suddenly broken by two gunshots and the sound of frantic screaming, followed by coarse laughter. The new sheriff and deputy ran toward the noise, which came from an alley between the Roman Holiday Saloon and a gunsmith shop.

"That's Solley!" As the two lawmen entered the alley, Clay Adams pointed to a thin, almost emaciated man wearing a blue coat of the Union Army.

Solley was standing with his back against the wall of the saloon. Two men were standing in front of him with their guns drawn. "Come on Solley, dance some more for us."

"Yeah," said the other man, who aimed his six-shooter in the direction of Solley's right foot. "Pretend you're dancin' for old Abe Lincoln hisself."

"Don'tcha say nothin' bad 'bout Abraham Lincoln. He was a great man!" Solley screamed. He sounded like a child throwing a tantrum.

"Then I think you should dance for the great man."

"That's enough!" Matheson yelled as he and Adams approached the three men. "Holster those guns."

The man who was aiming his gun at Solley's foot

turned his head and sneered. "Well, the new sheriff and his new deputy. I'll bet the sheriff wants to make Solley a deputy too."

"What's wrong with you, Ross Huett?" Clay asked angrily. "Everyone knows what a fine man Solley was before he went to the war. And now that he's not right in the head, and his family's all gone—the least you can do is treat the man decent."

"You're a good one to talk about actin' decent." Ross didn't move his gun. "The boss gave you a job and you repaid him by becoming a traitor."

"Holster the guns!" Matheson repeated. "I'm not going to say it again."

Huett's eyes shifted to Matheson. "Your guns are already holstered. Think you can shoot us before we get you?"

"Yes."

Solley's tormentors hesitated, not knowing what to do. Four men stood in the alley motionless, watching each other intently. Almost forgotten, Solley leaned against the Roman Holiday mumbling, "Abraham Lincoln was a great man, a great man . . ."

Ross Huett holstered his gun and his partner immediately followed. Huett looked directly at Clay Adams. "You're gonna be sorry you ever turned your back on Bull Grady. This is his town, and you're gonna learn that real soon."

The two gunmen hurried off. Both lawmen turned their attention to Solley. Matheson noted that the man's Union coat was tattered and no longer had any buttons.

"Those jaspers are gone now, Solley," Adams spoke in a low, comforting voice. "They won't bother you no more."

"Go to church!" Solley screamed again. He was still terrified. "I want to go to church!"

"What's he talking about?" Matheson asked.

"When Solley gets scared, he likes to stay in the church. It's the one place where he knows nobody will pick on him. The reverend gives him a little money to clean the place up. Solley likes to sleep in the pews. He feels safe there."

Matheson looked carefully at the sad individual in front of him. Solley looked like he hadn't had a restful sleep in several days. "Let's walk with him to the church," the sheriff said. "I think Solley's had enough troubles for a while."

As they approached the church, they saw Reverend Stubby about to enter the building. The pastor heard them coming, turned and waved. As he did, they could hear scampering feet behind them.

"Preacher! Preacher! You gotta come quick!" The boy almost collided with Matheson's left leg as he ran by him.

"That's Caleb Webb," Adams said. "His folks have a place a few miles from here. Wonder what's botherin' him."

Matheson sighed. "I've got an idea it's more bad news."

Chapter Eleven

Threatening shouts and curses cut the air as Reverend Stubby and Caleb Webb rode toward the Webb farm. "That's my pa. Sorry 'bout his cursing, Reverend."

The nine year old boy's voice sounded sad and re-signed. Frank Stuben wanted to say something encouraging to the lad, but now wasn't the time for it. "Caleb, can you still crawl through that little window at the back of your cabin?"

"Yes, sir. I don't fit easy no more, but I can still do it. Did it once already. That's how I got away to come get you."

The pastor and Caleb were now drawing close to the Webb cabin. Tom Webb, a tall, scrawny man, was pounding angrily on the door. "You open up, Lizzy. I got me an ax, now. Don't make me use it. If I have to break down this door, I'll whup you good!"

"Your Pa is going to spot us soon," The clergyman spoke in a calm voice. "I want you to ride fast to the back of the cabin and crawl inside. Tell your ma I'm out here."

"But—"

"Your ma will feel safer having you there with her. Now, ride!"

Caleb did as he was told. The pastor felt relieved. Tom Webb had enough problems. Humiliating him in front of his son would devastate the man.

"I'm givin' you one last chance, Lizzy." Tom stopped and spotted Caleb riding to the back of the cabin, then he turned and shouted at the newcomer. "You git outta here now! This ain't none of your concern!"

Reverend Stubby rode until he was a few feet from the man who had ordered him to leave. He reigned in his horse and spoke softly. "This *is* my concern. You know that, Tom."

Webb lifted the ax in one hand and walked toward the pastor. "You ride out, now, or I'll plant this ax in your head."

Reverend Stubby waited until his adversary was inches away and then delivered a fast kick to his wrist; the ax spiraled to the ground.

"You little runt." Tom Webb rubbed his wrist and gave the weapon a quick glance.

"Leave the ax where it is, Tom." Stuben's voice remained calm and low.

"I'd like to see you git off that horse and say that to me."

The pastor immediately dismounted. "Leave the ax where it is, Tom. You don't need an ax to talk with me or to talk with your wife and son. And you don't need the drink."

"A man's entitled—"

The parson suddenly raised his voice. "A man's not entitled to anything that turns him into a fool and makes him hurt his own family."

"Caleb had no right—"

"Caleb did exactly what was right. He saw you drinking out in the barn. He knew what that stuff does to you."

"He stole my bottle when I put it down."

"The boy didn't steal anything," the clergyman shot back. "He took the bottle back to the cabin and gave it to his ma. It should have ended there. But you came storming after Caleb, threatening to beat him and his mother. You forced your own wife and son to bolt the door against you."

Tom paused and looked at the ground, then at the sky. Neither view seemed to make him happy. "You don't understand, things ain't gone the way we planned . . ."

"They never do, Tom. That's why it's important to remember that we're not the ones running the show. I've talked to you a lot about prayer, have you given that any kind of a chance?"

Tom Webb shook his head.

"Tom, that bottle has separated you from your wife, your son, and your God. But you could make all three of those folks very happy right now."

"How's that?"

"You know how." A silence followed as the pastor gave Tom Webb a hard, uncompromising stare.

Tom's hands trembled as he started to knock on the cabin door. He looked pleadingly at Reverend Stubby. The pastor rapped his knuckles on the heavy wood. "Lizzy, Tom and I need to come inside."

The door opened and the two men entered. Lizzy Webb, a slight, pretty woman, worked her hands nervously and Caleb was watching wide-eyed. Tom tried to look at them but couldn't; his eyes were fixed on the bottle which now sat on the family dinner table. A bottle which was almost three quarters full. Tom suddenly grabbed the whiskey and ran out the open door. Moments after he vanished, a crashing sound came from the side of the cabin.

As the pastor, Lizzy, and Caleb ran outdoors, they saw Tom holding the neck of a shattered bottle in his hand. "The angels are rejoicing," Reverend Stubby whispered as Lizzy and Caleb ran to embrace Tom Webb.

The sun was low but bright as the parson turned for a final glance at the Webb farm. All three members of the family were making their way slowly inside the cabin.

Reverend Frank Stuben rode at a brisk pace toward town and thought about the Webbs. Tom had taken an important first step. He showed that he truly wanted to give up the drink. He had promised to never ride into town alone, where the temptation to buy a bottle was so powerful. "I sure thought that being elected mayor was important," the clergyman said to his buckskin as he patted him on the neck, "but I need to remember that my first calling is to help people like Tom Webb."

A shot missed the pastor by inches. His horse neighed and started to bolt. Reverend Stubby quickly gained control of the animal as he drew his revolver and fired in the direction of a lone boulder that perched at the side of the road.

There was nowhere to take cover. The pastor would have to battle the ambusher from open space. Sunlight flashed from one side of the large rock and Reverend Stubby fired two more shots in that direction.

The shots ricocheted off the boulder, causing the bushwhacker to lose his balance and fall. As he hit the ground, his Winchester twirled out of his hand and out of reach.

Reverend Stubby turned his horse and charged directly at his assailant. The shooter glanced quickly at the rifle then ran to his horse and spurred the sorrel into a fast gallop.

The sorrel was a strong animal and the bushwhacker was able to put some territory between himself and his pursuer. But the land was flat and Reverend Stubby kept the outlaw in easy view. The fleeing gunman seemed to drop off the earth for a moment, then reappeared with splashes of water cascading behind him.

As Reverend Stubby charged through the shallow stream, he saw his prey take a split in the road that led toward a thicket of tall, reed-like trees at the edge of a rocky canyon. Riding hard, the outlaw suddenly turned and fired two shots at the pastor, who ducked down instinctively.

Reverend Stubby took the split in the road and followed as a maze of branches and scraggly limbs seemed to swallow the gunman. In the trees, the road quickly narrowed and the pastor was forced to slow his horse, losing sight of the gunman. Urging the buckskin on as briskly as possible, he again came into range of the sorrel, but the horse had slowed to a light casual trot. Its rider had dismounted.

Frank Stuben stared for a moment at the riderless horse, then was hit by the realization that he had ridden into a trap. He cut his horse to the right and nudged him into a jump. The buckskin cleared a row of bushes near the canyon wall as gunshots sounded from the opposite side of the trail. Reverend Stubby tied the horse to a thin tree, grabbed his Winchester and some cartridges from the saddle, then took refuge behind a large rock.

At first, Reverend Stubby let the rifle lie. He hastily reloaded his revolver and began to respond to the shots that slammed against the rock from three different locations. That ploy only slowed down the attackers.

They were a patient bunch. They had their target pinned down and they knew it.

"Pride." Reverend Stubby whispered that word to himself like it was a curse. "You preach against pride, Stuben, but weren't you proud when you got that shooter to run."

Frank Stuben now saw that there had been a carefully prepared plan to kill him. If the bushwhacker failed, he was to lead his target into the canyon where two other gunmen were also waiting.

"Those two shots he fired while I crossed the stream were signals for his buddies," the pastor continued to mumble to himself. "But I was so proud for making a man almost twice my size run."

Another stream of bullets smashed against the rock. This was no time for reflection. Reverend Stubby picked up the Winchester and, firing as quickly as he could, sprayed ammunition in three directions. That bought him a moment of quiet. His enemies were probably reloading and moving in closer.

The pastor slumped against the rock, then backed away from the intense heat coming from the stone. That small incident gave him an inspiration, it was a dangerous idea but Frank Stuben wasn't a man with a lot of choices.

He found an appropriate branch nearby: long, heavy enough to throw far, and like the rest of the wood and leaves in that thicket, very dry. He felt the matches in his shirt pocket as the next attack began. These shots were closer and accompanied by laughter and curses that were hurled in his direction. He fired back with his revolver, inducing more shots and yelps.

Another silence. They were closing in. The pastor quickly reloaded his Colt, holstered it and grabbed the branch. He lit one end with a match, then stood and hurled the fiery branch across the trail to the thickets where his enemies were hiding.

Frank Stuben had seen wildfires before, but was still shocked by how quickly the flames spread. He could hear the panicked neighing of horses and the shouts of terrified men as the flames rampaged across the thicket. That fire was monstrously hungry and would soon be after him. The buckskin was trying to break loose as Reverend Stubby returned his Winchester to the saddle. He untied the reigns and hoisted onto the horse with one motion. The buckskin was near panic as the pastor guided him between bushes and the canyon wall, away from the flames. At a break in the brush, the horse took off with a frenzied gallop back along the narrow road. Reverend Stubby could hear the sound of other hooves galloping in the opposite direction.

The buckskin kept up a fast run as the trail widened. Frank Stuben guided his horse toward a scraggly bush that sided the stream. He pulled up the skittish animal and tied his reigns to the bush. The clergyman yanked a bandana from his pocket, tied it around the buckskin's eyes and hoped the animal wouldn't bolt. He pulled the Winchester from the saddle's scabbard and slipped a cartridge into the rifle. He dropped a few more cartridges into his pocket, gave the horse a re-assuring pat, then lay flat on the ground.

After several minutes it became obvious that his ears had been right; the assailants had ridden off in the opposite direction and they weren't coming back.

Reverend Stubby got to his feet and returned his Winchester to the saddle. "Those owlhoots will circle around and head back to town," he said to the buck-skin. "That way they can try to kill me again tonight."

The pastor looked at the ground, feeling drained and numb. He couldn't keep on; always being the one who was encouraging, always laughing about his size so other folks wouldn't feel bad when they laughed about it and all the time fighting for civilization in an unta-med, brutal land.

His eyes shifted to the stream, and that long ago day appeared to him once again, that day when he sat in the office of the college president, Dr. Harold Whit-worth. Dr. Whitworth was a distinguished looking man with iron gray hair and a gentle British accent.

They had been discussing a scholarly paper on one of the Old Testament prophets, authored by Frank Stu-ben. Dr. Whitworth suddenly changed the subject. "Frank, I urge you to forget this romantic dream of yours about returning to the Arizona Territory. You belong in the east, where you can pursue the life of a scholar. You have wonderful gifts that are appreciated here, whereas in the west . . ."

Frank Stuben finished the thought: "The only thing people will care about there is that I'm very short."

Dr. Whitworth looked embarrassed and stammered a bit. "You can have a normal life here, a good life. Please, Frank, reconsider your decision."

"The decision was not mine, Dr. Whitworth. God has called me to return home and start a church."

The pastor picked up a pebble and skimmed it across the water trying to chase off the memory, without success. For the first time, he thought that maybe the college president had been right. If he had stayed in the east he would now be Professor Stuben instead of Reverend Stubby. He would be a respected scholar who spoke at academic gatherings instead of a trouble-making preacher who had a gang of outlaws trying to kill him.

Loud crackling sounds of fire emanated from the thicket which was now burning into oblivion. The noise caused the pastor to turn and walk slowly toward the blaze. He stopped when the heat began to envelope him.

The Lord had spoken to Moses through fire, the pastor thought. Moses, a man of eighty, who couldn't speak without stuttering, was called by God to stand against a powerful despot. Moses resisted the call at first, but he did what the Lord commanded and a people became free.

The pastor's eyes remained fixed on the erratic movement of the flames as he pondered how Moses had actually heard the voice of God. Even so, he thought, the great leader was not always content with his lot in life, now and then he felt sorry for himself, just like I do sometimes.

Reverend Stubby dropped to his knees on the rocky sand and bowed his head. He didn't really know how much time had passed when he got up and walked with renewed energy back to his horse.

The buckskin was calm now and straining his head to reach the water in the stream. "You're entitled to some refreshment, fella," Reverend Stubby said as he removed the bandana from the horse's eyes and untethered him. "We all need some refreshment from time to time."

The clergyman took his canteen from the saddle, took a fast swig, then looked back at the fire. This time a look of determination covered his face. "But we can't take too long, good friend. There's a lot of work to be done."

A few minutes later, he returned the canteen to the saddle, mounted, and rode directly back to town.

Chapter Twelve

Boyd Matheson tried to keep his cough subdued and under control. He didn't quite succeed, but everyone's attention remained focused on Reverend Stubby, who was explaining how three gunmen had tried to kill him only a couple of hours before.

Almost everyone. Matheson saw Laurel Remick staring intently at him with concern, and something else he couldn't identify. Laurel's behavior toward him had seemed a bit strange since he arrived at Remick's General Store that evening for the town council meeting.

The sheriff had to cough again. Again, no one paid attention except Laurel. The young woman pressed her lips together and it appeared that her eyes were getting moist. That could be because of all the smoke that clouded the store, Matheson figured; still . . .

The lawman shifted his attention to Laurel's father, who was asking a question. ". . . how do you figure they knew you were out at the Webb place?"

Reverend Stubby shrugged his shoulders. "I wasn't at the church when Caleb rode into town. He had to ask around for me. The boy was upset, of course, and he was speaking in a loud voice. A lot of people saw us ride out of town together."

The pastor glanced at Boyd Matheson, then looked at the other council members sitting around the long table. "Our sheriff has informed me that tonight he will be taking special precautions to keep me alive. Not that I'm entitled to special treatment. But tomorrow is election day and a meaningful election requires at least two candidates. Boyd Matheson wants to do all he can to make sure that is the case."

A scattering of laughter followed the last remark. The pastor nodded in Matheson's direction as he sat down. "I'll let the sheriff take over the meeting now."

Matheson got to his feet, quickly cleared his throat and began to speak. "Bull Grady knows he has to kill Reverend Stubby tonight. Otherwise, he loses the election. But with Reverend Stubby gone, well . . ."

"You don't have to feel bad 'bout sayin' it," Hank Mellor boomed. "The reverend has been the ramrod of this outfit. Take him away and there ain't no fire in the furnace. Reckon Bull Grady knows that too."

Cassius Remick nodded his head and spoke to the sheriff. "Maybe we should hide the pastor somewhere, or get him out of town."

"Grady's got more men than us. We've already learned that it's dangerous for Reverend Stubby to leave town. We can't avoid a fight. Grady won't let us. We need to take a stand here and do it right now. This town either belongs to Bull Grady or to the rest of us," Matheson said. "We'll guard the reverend at the church, or maybe in his home—"

"It's the same place," the clergyman interrupted. Matheson looked a bit confused.

"I live in the church," the reverend explained. "There's a cot in my office where I sleep."

"We don't pay our preachers too good," Cassius Remick added.

"The church will be fine." Matheson hastily continued. "Deputy Clay Adams and me will stay with Reverend Stubby. The other place that needs guarding is this place, Remick's General Store."

"Why's that?" Orin Mellor asked.

"Deputy Adams hasn't wasted any time since taking on his duties. Tell them what you learned, Clay."

Clay Adams remained seated. He was nervous, but still a bit pleased at being the center of attention. "As everone knows, the store here is where the votin' will take place tomorrow. I looked up the ordinance about that. There has to be a ten day advance notice sayin' where the votin's gonna be."

Adams looked around the table and saw that not everyone was following him. "Don't you see? If this place were to burn down or somethin' tonight, it would be another ten days before we could have the election. Ten days ain't much, but right now Bull Grady is desperate to try anythin'. We've got to protect this store."

Smiles of approval fired in Clay Adams' direction. That made the sheriff almost as pleased as the deputy.

"This store is going to be the second area we protect." Matheson again was speaking. "Cassius and Laurel will be here, along with the doc and Orin and Hank Mellor. The doc and Laurel will be tending to the wounded. I'm afraid they might have a busy night."

"May I say something, Sheriff," Doc Evans interrupted.

"Sure, go ahead."

Doctor Rufus Evans slowly looked around the table. His voice was steady and his demeanor calm. "Tonight I will attend to every wounded soul that is brought to me. I will give our people my attention first. But everyone will be cared for. Nobody will be neglected and allowed to die just because they're not on our side. That is the way it is going to be."

Matheson and Reverend Stubby exchanged quick smiles of encouragement. Matheson wondered if maybe the same thing that had allowed him to throw his tobacco out the window hadn't gotten into Doc Evans. Tonight, the doctor certainly didn't look like a man who was struggling with alcohol.

Matheson glanced at everyone sitting around him. "You heard the man. He's the doctor." There was another factor that the sheriff didn't mention. Rufus

Evans was the town's only doctor. A man everyone needed. Matheson hoped that Grady's men would be reluctant to harm the doc directly or to try and burn down the store he was working in.

"Any more questions?" The sheriff looked quickly around the table. "Meeting dismissed," he said.

Clay Adams approached the sheriff and spoke in a near whisper. "Somethin's botherin' me about all this."

"Yeah?" Matheson replied.

"I've lived in this town all my life. Heard folks say plenty of bad things about Bull Grady. But I never heard anybody say he wasn't smart."

"So?"

"I think Grady is usin' that head of his. I think he's got somethin' planned. Somethin' we ain't thought about. Trouble is, I ain't got no idea what that plan is."

Matheson nodded his head. "Know what you mean. I don't know exactly what Grady is up to, and that worries me."

Chapter Thirteen

Clay Adams, Reverend Stubby, and Boyd Matheson stood in front of the double doors of the Gradyville Community Church. "Clay, you go to church here. You should know the place. I want you to go in and scout around. Almost everyone in town knows that the reverend lives here. It would be an obvious place to lay a trap for him. Make sure none of Grady's boys are waiting inside. I'll stay here with the reverend."

"I think we can all go in together, that way—"

"I'm just being cautious, Reverend." The sheriff knew that Reverend Stubby was embarrassed by having so much fuss made over his safety. He'd just have to put up with it until the election was over.

The deputy entered the church carrying a Winchester. He quickly lit a kerosene lamp on the back wall beside the double doors. He then lit an identical lamp on the other side of the entrance.

There was enough light to view about a quarter of the church. The building didn't afford many hiding places. There were eight pews on each side, split by an aisle which ran down the middle of the sanctuary. There was also an aisle on each side of the pews. Adams couldn't detect any movement, but the front of the church remained very dark.

Adams moved cautiously down the right aisle. When he reached the third pew from the front, he spotted a lump lying in the pew near the center aisle. As he entered the row and moved toward the figure he could hear a vague mumbling: "Abraham Lincoln . . . man . . . great man . . ."

Clay Adams smiled sadly and left Solley to his dreams. Maybe sleep was the only contentment Solley knew. Let him enjoy it while he could.

Adams quietly slithered around the pew and continued to look over the church. He lit the kerosene lamps on the sides and in the front, then looked behind the pulpit and in the pastor's study. Typical of most churches, the pulpit and choir loft were on a slightly elevated platform. The deputy made his way to the top row of the choir loft which afforded a good view of the church. He spotted nothing troublesome. The lights had not bothered Solley. The gentle up and down of his blue coat indicated that the man was sleeping soundly. Adams laughed softly to himself. As hard as those pews were, he couldn't figure out how anyone could sleep in one.

Adams quickly returned to the double doors and opened them. "All clear!" Matheson and the pastor scooted in.

The sheriff did a quick survey of the church. "There's a window on each side big enough for a man to crawl through," he observed, then pointed behind him. "Are there any other ways in or out of this church?"

"No, that's it," Reverend Stubby answered.

"Is there any spare lumber around here, something we could run through the handles of the doors? I'd like to make things tough on anyone who might get some ideas about barging into this place."

"There are a few old logs in my office."

"Let's take a look."

The three men moved down the center aisle toward the pastor's study which was located beside the pulpit. Matheson was thinking that they had found a good location for protecting Gradyville's next mayor. The church had strong walls, only two windows, and one entrance. Not a bad setup for a fortress.

These thoughts lasted until they reached the pastor's study. "I want all three of you gents to stop and put up your hands, or I'll kill all of you right now," a stern voice commanded.

The three men did what they were told.

"Now, turn around and walk slow until all three of you are standin' in front of that pulpit."

As they turned around Matheson recognized Ross Huett, the man who had been tormenting Solley earlier in the day. Huett was standing in the third pew and wearing Solley's blue coat. Matheson wondered what had happened to Solley. He assumed that Huett had been posing as Solley and gave a few angry thoughts as to why his deputy hadn't checked "Solley" a little more carefully.

There were more immediate problems to worry about. Huett was obviously a part of a larger plan. One man couldn't be expected to hold three for a long period of time, not three men who knew anything about guns. Huett would be able to shoot one of them, maybe two, but he would take a bullet himself. The church was probably surrounded by Bull Grady's men waiting for a signal to enter.

The sheriff, his deputy, and the pastor stood in a line in front of the pulpit, facing Huett. Matheson was in the middle. "Okay," Huett said, "very slow-like I want all three of you to take off your guns and drop them to the floor."

Matheson nodded to his two companions to obey. But he knew that the order had to be defied. Once they were unarmed, Huett would fire a signal and the place would be filled with Grady's men. That meant death for all three of them.

Huett's hand was shaking. He was the key man in this plan and didn't want to botch it. Matheson noticed that Huett's eyes bounced from him to Adams. Ross Huett paid only scant attention to the pastor who stood on Matheson's right.

Matheson quickly touched the pastor with his arm. Huett didn't seem to catch the movement.

"You too, Sheriff, take off your gun!" Ross Huett shouted from the pew.

"I don't plan to jump, just because you say so." Without being too conspicuous about it, Matheson put some emphasis on the word *jump*.

"I mean it, right now or . . ."

Matheson spoke in low voice heavy with challenge: "Earlier today, you had your gun pointed at the ground and I told you I could draw fast enough to shoot you before you could do me any harm."

"So?"

"Right now, you've got a gun pointed right at me," Matheson said. "I think I can still outdraw you."

"That's crazy!" Adams shouted.

"We'll see about that. On three." Matheson's eyes rolled to his deputy. "Start counting."

"No, Sheriff, this ain't right. Huett's a hired gun, he—"

"Start counting." Matheson was happy that Reverend Stubby remained silent. That was a good sign, one of the few good signs the lawman had going for him.

"One," Clay counted. Matheson's right hand hovered over his six-shooter. Huett aimed directly at his adversary's chest.

"Two," Clay continued to count. Reverend Stubby hopped onto the front pew and jumped toward Ross Huett. Huett turned his gun toward the apparition that was hurtling toward him. Matheson drew and fired.

Huett staggered backward and got off one shot at the pastor before dropping to the floor. Reverend Stubby yelled in pain before colliding hard with the pew and landing on top of the hired gun who had shot him.

The front doors of the church banged open and two men tried to run in. Clay Adams grabbed his Winchester from the floor and brought down the first man. Adams quickly slammed another cartridge into the chamber of the rifle, but missed on the next try as the second man pulled his comrade from the building.

A barrage of bullets shattered the glass from the windows on both sides of the church. Matheson belly-crawled to the third pew and spotted Reverend Stubby on the floor tearing his shirt. "The bullet didn't enter," the preacher's voice sounded clear. "Ross Huett is dead; your shot got him right in the heart."

Matheson crawled to the pastor and examined the gash in his left arm. The wound was deep and bleeding. Matheson ripped strips of cloth from the clergyman's shirt and tied them around the wound. "Is that too tight?"

"No, I still have circulation. It should stop the bleeding, or slow it anyway."

"Can you take the left window?" Matheson asked.

"Sure can."

"Clay and me will take the other window and make sure no one comes in through the door." Matheson scooted through the pew until he reached a side window where Clay Adams had turned out the light beside the window and was cautiously glancing outside.

"I'll take care of things here," the sheriff said. "Turn out the rest of the lights, then go to the pastor's study and grab one of those logs. Bar the door."

"Sure. Ah . . . sorry about not takin' a closer look—"

"You'll get plenty of chances to make up for it before this night is done. Get moving!"

As Clay followed orders, Matheson looked out at some of the rustling shrubbery, about thirty yards from the church. He fired his six-shooter then jumped back, ducking a barrage of shots.

That move accomplished its aim. The shots came from two directions at the left and right of the window. Grady's men almost certainly had an identical set up on the other side of the church.

They wouldn't be in too big a hurry. Ross Huett was dead and another one of their men was, at least, seriously wounded. They would move in at a slow but steady pace. When they thought they had everyone inside busy holding them off, they'd send a group to break through the front doors.

Boyd Matheson glanced at the entrance. Adams had just finished ramming a log through the handles of the double doors. That will give us a couple extra minutes, Matheson thought grimly to himself.

The sheriff's attention shifted to the other side of the church where Reverend Stubby was carrying a Henry rifle from his office to the window. He then duplicated Matheson's maneuver with exactly the same results. Shots came through the window from both the right and left.

"Be careful of the crossfire!" Stuben yelled to his companions. Matheson noticed that the pastor's hands were steady but his face was becoming increasingly pale.

Clay Adams returned to the window, glanced through it briefly, then fired his Winchester to the right. A torrent of shots plowed through the window and burrowed into the far wall of the church. Matheson replied with three shots to the left from his Colt. A loud screech of pain sounded from the bushes outside.

"You got one of them, Sheriff!" Fresh confidence streaked across the deputy's face.

Boyd Matheson smiled and nodded. He wanted to keep that confidence there. But he knew the reason why one of his bullets had found its mark. Grady's men were advancing faster than he had thought. Soon, they would try again to break through the doors and invade the church.

Once again, shots sounded from outside. But these shots were different. They came from a shotgun and were not aimed at the church. Another anguished scream came from one of Grady's men.

"The Mellors!" Reverend Stubby shouted. "One of them is on each side of the church, firing at the enemy."

"Ain't nobody anywhere better with a shotgun then

Hank Mellor," Clay said. "Except maybe Orin. Hank taught his boy good."

The tenor of the battle changed immediately. The attackers became the attacked and some responded by taking off. All of Grady's men stopped advancing. They had to retreat in order to fight off the new arrivals while battling the barrage of bullets that continued to assault them from the church.

The defections from Grady's private army increased. Soon, shouts of "stop shootin', we surrender!" came from both sides of the church.

The three men ran outside to aid the Mellors. There were eight of Grady's men left and two of them were wounded. The victors ordered their healthy captives to the ground, where their hands could be tied.

A loud yelp sounded from the direction of Remick's General Store. "Perkins," Matheson said out loud. "Something has happened to Perkins!" He turned to his deputy. "Take charge here."

A horrible anger filled Boyd Matheson as he ran toward the general store. All of that anger was directed at himself. Grady had outsmarted them. He forced them to use most of their power at the church, then he attacked the general store.

Matheson's chest felt like a hot branding iron was pressing against it, but he couldn't cut his speed. He didn't know what had happened at the store, but he did know that Perkins would attack anyone who tried to harm Laurel.

When Matheson ran into the store he saw Doc

Evans on his knees attending to Cassius Remick who lay on a flour sack. Cassius had blood running down one side of his head.

Matheson started to ask a question but his voice came out a wheeze.

"The Tibbs brothers, the ones who make the tanglefoot, came here, a few minutes ago." As Rufus Evans spoke, Matheson noticed that his right eye was swelling. "They overpowered Cassius and me and took Laurel. They're traveling in that buckboard of theirs. Use my claybank at the hitching post outside. The horse is fresh.

"How many horses on their buckboard?"

"Four. They can make good time."

Boyd Matheson nodded and ran for the claybank. As he mounted, he caught a quick glance of Perkins lying beside the store. The dog was obviously in pain. Matheson hoped Perkins wasn't dying but had no time to help him.

The claybank seemed restless and welcomed a chance to run. On the outskirts of town Matheson spotted the outline of the buckboard against the light of a bright moon. The sharp clanging noises coming from the old wagon didn't slow the claybank.

The buckboard swayed across the road that weaved out of town. Waves of dust streamed behind it. Matheson pulled his bandana over his nose and hunched down as the claybank steadily caught up with the dilapidated wagon. The horse wasn't timid. He didn't slow down or become jittery as he pulled up beside the buckboard. Dust and tears blurred Matheson's vision, but looking into the wagon he could see Abner Tibbs straighten his derby then pick up a rifle.

Matheson glanced at Dencel Tibbs driving the rig. The lawman couldn't spot Laurel and had no time to look for her through the dust. He slipped both feet out of the stirrups and leaped toward Abner Tibbs. Matheson collided with Abner, and the weapon flew out of his hands as it discharged a shot into the air. Both men slammed onto the floor of the buckboard, then scrambled onto their feet.

Dencil Tibbs halted the wagon. Horses squealed as the wagon bumped across the road, almost turned over, and both men were again thrown down and had to roll back onto their feet. This time, Abner Tibbs lost his derby but regained his rifle.

Grabbing the gun by its barrel, Abner swung it like a club. Matheson ducked and landed a punch to his attacker's gut. Abner Tibbs staggered and fell from the wagon, dropping the rifle when he hit the ground. He began a fast crawl toward the gun. Matheson pulled his Colt and fired a shot that hit the rifle and gave it a half spin in the dust.

From the corner of his eye, Matheson spotted a figure moving at him from behind. The lawman twirled and smashed Dencel Tibbs in the jaw with his revolver. As Dencel dropped to his knees, Matheson grabbed his right arm and hurled him off the buckboard. He hit the ground beside his brother. Both men were now in comfortable range of the Colt.

"Stay right where you are, both of you!" They obeyed, and Boyd Matheson used the moment to locate Laurel. She was lying bound and gagged at the back of the wagon, or she had been. Laurel had managed to free her hands and was now untying the knots that held her ankles.

The sheriff turned back to the two squalid men who were now on their feet and looking at him sheepishly, like naughty boys standing in front of the schoolmarm. Abner Tibbs smiled in a manner that was both charming and threatening. "Nice to meet up with you ag'in Sheriff Matheson. Even things bein' the way they are, I do have a favor to ask."

Matheson's eyes briefly flashed to Laurel Remick. She was now on her feet, untying the gag that was in her mouth. As she looked down at the Tibbs brothers her face reflected a deep anger, a fire which he had not seen since his first hour in Gradyville. That fire wasn't there because of what the Tibbs' had done to her, these men had beaten her father and Doctor Evans and hurt Perkins, possibly killing the animal.

"What might that favor be?" Matheson asked, happy that this time, his words didn't come out in a wheeze. He'd had adequate time to regain some of his breath.

"Could ya throw me down my derby? Sounds kinda crazy, but ya know, I jus' don't feel like a whole man 'less I got that fool thing on my head."

Matheson picked up the derby and ripped out the small derringer that was sewed into a pocket in the lining. He carefully inspected the rest of the hat for weapons, then twirled it down to Abner Tibbs. "I think your derby will fit a mite more comfortably now."

"Obliged, Sheriff." Abner smiled in a resigned manner as he picked up the hat and placed it on his head.

"I know you gents are a bit out of practice, but I want to hear the truth from you. It will be in your best interest to speak the truth."

"Now, Dencel and me is just po' farm boys." Abner carefully straightened his derby, like he was about to depart for a dance. "You're gonna have to explain things to us, make it simple-like."

"Bull Grady can't protect you anymore; the king has fallen," Matheson said. He hoped he was right. "Grady will soon be attending another trial, this time as the defendant. If you're smart, you'll tell everything you know about the man. If you're willing to testify against Bull Grady, the circuit judge will be a lot more favorable when it comes time to decide your punishment."

As he spoke, Matheson hopped down from the wagon, then held Laurel's hand as she did the same. All of the time, he kept his Colt fixed on the Tibbs brothers. When he had stopped speaking, Laurel whispered an anxious, "Are you okay?" Matheson replied with a fast, "Sure, how 'bout you?" Laurel nodded her head and flashed a wistful smile.

The quick exchange bothered Matheson, but he couldn't give it much thought. He gave the Tibbs brothers an intense stare, waiting for their reply to his last remark.

"Guess I should explain that Dencel don't talk much," Abner Tibbs said. "Havin' me for a brother he don't really need to. So, ask your questions, Sheriff. I'll answer jus' like I had my hand on the good book."

"Did Bull Grady pay you to kidnap Laurel Remick?"

"Kid her 'bout wha—"

"Did Grady pay you to grab Laurel Remick tonight and take her away against her will?"

"He surely did," Abner Tibbs beamed, "a hunert dollars up front and another hunert when the work was done. Another two hunert if we had to kill her."

Boyd Matheson tried to contain his excitement. He might have testimony that could convict Grady in a court of law. "You couldn't hide her at your place, too many people know where that is. Where were you taking her?"

"There's a cave here 'round abouts. Dencil and I knows it, but not too many other folks."

"Did Grady tell you why he wanted you to do all this?"

"Nope. Bull Grady gives orders. He never explains nothin.' "

"What were you supposed to do with Laurel Remick once you got her to the cave?"

"Give her grub and drink enough to keep her alive. Grady tole us that Pete Wheeler would come out and tell us what to do. We was only to take orders from Pete."

"That's enough questions for now." Matheson

turned to Laurel. "Could you fetch the rope from the claybank? I am going to tie up these gentlemen real tight. Wouldn't want anything to happen to our star witnesses."

Laurel Remick drove the wagon back to town. Matheson sat beside her, ready in case the Tibbs brothers began to cause trouble. That didn't appear likely. Matheson had carefully checked both men to make sure they had no weapons on them before he tied them up in the back of the buckboard.

Matheson noticed that Laurel handled the team of horses well, though it was apparent she didn't drive a wagon often. He also noticed that she appeared pensive and troubled. He wished that he could give her some reassuring news about her father and Perkins but he really didn't know how they were and didn't want to give her false hope.

"It looks like this terrible night is almost over." Laurel said as they entered town.

Matheson looked around him. Everything appeared calm. He once again glanced at the Tibbs brothers, then at Doc Evans' claybank which was tied to the buckboard.

"Almost over," he said. "Still something that needs to be done."

"What?"

"I have to arrest Bull Grady," the sheriff said.

Chapter Fourteen

Laurel Remick stopped the wagon in front of the sheriff's office. Matheson took it as a good sign when Clay Adams stepped out to meet them. The deputy would not be in the office if there was still serious trouble in town.

The two lawmen unloaded the wagon's cargo, then Laurel hastily drove off toward Remick's General Store. The Tibbs brothers joined six other prisoners who were housed in two of the four jail cells that made up the back of the sheriff's office.

"We've got two more prisoners over at the general store," Clay Adams reported as he closed the door on the cell area. "They won't cause no problems for some time. Shot up pretty bad, but they'll live to get their day in court."

"Where's the reverend?"

"He's at the store. The doc patched up the reverend's arm and Mr. Remick's head. Both of the Mellors are there too, just in case Bull Grady gets any more fool notions."

"Did you find Solley?"

Clay Adams looked at the floor, then, with some effort looked at his boss. "Solley was lyin' behind the church. He'd been beat up bad and hog tied. But Doc says Solley will be okay. He's restin' at the store now."

Boyd Matheson wanted to ask about Perkins, but felt embarrassed to do so. "Guess I'll drop by the store for a bit." He started toward the front door then turned around to his deputy. "Don't worry about falling for that trick. I mean Huett dressed as Solley and all. I've been fooled by tricks a lot dumber than that. You've gotta get fooled now and again. That's the only way to get smart."

Adams smiled and nodded as his boss left the office.

As the sheriff walked toward the General Store he noticed that Gradyville was quiet, but not really peaceful. There was a feeling of tension and uncertainty in the humid Arizona night. Bull Grady's kingdom was in chaos but the king was still free. Until Grady was defeated and in jail, he would continue hold the town in a grip of fear.

Entering Remick's General Store, Matheson's eyes went immediately to Laurel, who was holding Perkins as a woman might hold an infant. She was talking softly to the animal as he wagged his tail and licked his mistress' face. The mongrel would have looked healthy except for the bandage that covered the left side of his head.

"Doc Evans made me wait until he had Perkins all patched up," Reverend Stubby shouted good-naturedly. "The doc said he'd rather hear that mongrel bark than me preach!"

Laughter cascaded over a scene of confusion and uncertainty. Two of Grady's men lay on the empty flour sacks that now covered much of the makeshift clinic. Their injuries were obviously serious but Clay Adams was right: they'd live to stand trial.

Solley was sitting in a chair singing softly to himself. He seemed content. Neither of the Mellors had been injured. Cassius Remick was walking in a cautious manner and moving his head slowly, but appeared to be doing okay. Like his canine patient, Doc Evans had a bandage on the left side of his head. But the doctor's gait was steady. Matheson couldn't tell how seriously injured Reverend Stubby was, and he knew that was exactly the way the pastor wanted it.

Boyd Matheson felt awkward. Everyone seemed to be looking at him, waiting for him to say something. He suddenly remembered one of the reasons he had come. "Orin, could you go over to the sheriff's office? We'll be needing you there in a bit."

"Sure." Orin nodded to everyone and left.

"Sheriff, I wanna thank—"

"It's a mite soon to be thanking anyone, yet," Matheson interrupted Cassius Remick. "Bull Grady still isn't in jail. And the only case we got against him rests on the testimony of the Tibbs brothers."

"We're going to win, Sheriff Matheson, we proved that tonight." Boyd Matheson looked curiously at Reverend Stubby; so did everyone else.

"I knew we had won tonight at the church, when the Mellors arrived and the battle started going our way." Reverend Stubby looked down at the two prisoners who were sleeping fitfully, then continued. "I watched Bull Grady's men. Many of them, the ones that could, ran off. They're riding hard, far away from Gradyville by now. The men inside that church would never run. We would have died there if that's what it took."

The pastor took a coin out of his pocket, tossed it in the air and caught it. "Grady's men are fighting for money, nothing more. If the fighting gets too tough, they'll leave and find someone else who will pay them to kill. We're fighting because this is our home. We belong here and no crook can take it away from us!"

There was a brief silence broken by Laurel's soft voice. "Thank you, Reverend Stuben, you just reminded us of some things we might have forgotten."

Boyd Matheson touched two fingers to his hat, nodded and walked outside. He stepped off the boardwalk and looked to the sky, wondering if this would be his last night on earth.

"Mr. Matheson?"

The sheriff turned to face Laurel Remick. The young woman laughed self consciously. "It seems that whenever you want a little time to yourself, I come along. Guess I'm nothing but a bother."

"You're never a bother, Miss Remick. No need to apologize."

Perkins walked from the store to his mistress' side. The mongrel twitched his head about as the young woman cautiously scratched the side of his right ear. "Doctor Evans says that bandage will probably itch a little."

She paused, then once again looked directly at the lawman. "I do need to apologize to you, Mr. Matheson; I've done a very rude thing."

Boyd Matheson laughed. "Sorry, Miss Remick, but after dealing with killers it sounded sort of funny to hear someone say they were sorry for being 'rude'."

"Mr. Matheson, I followed you last night when you went to see Doctor Evans. I hid by the window and listened. I know what the doctor said to you."

"Have you told anyone else?"

"No."

The lawmen felt very nervous. He remembered hearing Perkins bark outside of Doc Evans' window. "Well then, no real harm done, I guess. We can just keep this a secret between you, me, and Perkins." Matheson nodded at the dog, trying to make a joke.

"Mr. Matheson, it is not right. It's not right that a man who has done so much for this town should have to go through something like this alone." She took two steps toward him. "I know—"

"Do you believe in God, Miss Remick?"

The young woman retreated a step. The question had obviously stunned her. "Why, yes I do, Mr. Matheson, very much so."

"So do I." The lawman smiled, then continued. "I wouldn't have said that for certain a few days ago, but now I do believe, and that changes things."

"In what way?"

"I find myself thinking a lot more about the future, Miss Remick."

Laurel's voice carried confusion and concern. "You mean, your own future?"

"Yeah, a body can't help but think about that, but there's more to it. I've been thinking a lot about this town, too."

Boyd Matheson crouched down and began to fuss over Perkins. Laurel realized that the lawman was collecting his thoughts and remained quiet.

"The most important work that I'll ever do for this town will be all done after tonight—one way or another." Matheson gave the dog one last pat, then stood up.

"Gradyville will always need a sheriff," Laurel blurted out quickly.

"That's true enough. But it'll need other things even more." Matheson looked at the ground for a moment then faced the young woman. "This town is going to need builders. People to start families, keep the school and church going; people who can run stores, start ranches, and make this place really work."

This time Matheson looked to the sky and then back

at Laurel Remick. "Yeah, I've been thinking about the future, and I don't have all that much of it left. Not on this earth anyway. You need to start giving some thought to the future, Miss Remick. You are the kind of person this town really needs. More than it needs another fast gun."

They came together quickly and naturally. Boyd Matheson held the young woman as she sobbed quietly against his chest. When she slowly broke away from him she started to say something, then decided against it. Boyd Matheson watched in silence as Laurel picked up Perkins and lightly rubbed her face against his fur. Then she returned to the store and the many tasks that awaited her there.

Boyd Matheson turned and walked toward the sheriff's office. He also had a job to do.

Chapter Fifteen

Boyd Matheson and Clay Adams walked quickly toward the Fighting Bull Saloon. The deputy, as usual, was carrying a Winchester. "We could get Hank Mellor to come with us?" The tone of Adams' voice made the statement a question.

Matheson shook his head. "Orin is looking after the office. Cassius has been beat up pretty bad, he can't move too well, and I think the reverend may be hurt a bit worse than he lets on. We need Hank at the General Store."

Matheson shrugged his shoulders, then continued, "Besides, there's nothing here we can't handle."

"What do you think Grady is plannin'?"

The lawmen slowed their pace as they left the boardwalk and began to cross the street to the saloon. "Hard to say. Things are changing quick. Grady is

164

holed up in his office, he would feel safe there. Other—"

Matheson was pushed to the ground unexpectedly. As he hit dirt, he heard a shot explode from above. A quick glance up revealed a shadow moving on the roof of the Fighting Bull Saloon. The dark figure was crouched but suddenly bolted upright, preparing for another shot.

A rifle was fired, then the figure staggered and fell off the roof, plunging to the ground below. Matheson's eyes shifted to his left where Clay Adams was perched on one knee. The smoke from his Winchester gleamed briefly against the moon, then vanished.

Both lawmen jumped to their feet and ran to the wounded man. Matheson spoke as they crouched over the gunman, who was moaning a barely audible series of cries. "His holster is empty. All of his guns are probably up there on the roof. You know this jasper?"

"Calls himself Buck," the deputy replied. "Like most of the owlhoots who work for Bull Grady, he ain't much on handin' out his real name."

Matheson nodded, then gave Adams a crooked smile. "Mighty glad you're the watchful type."

"You should be thankin' Bull Grady."

"How's that?"

Adams looked down at the fallen gunman and retreated into his own thoughts, deciding whether or not to answer Matheson's question. After making up his mind, he looked at the sheriff and spoke in a voice laced with anger. " 'When I worked for him, Bull

Grady would talk to his main henchman, Pete Wheeler, forgettin' that I was even there. Guess the big man felt I wasn't worth payin' attention to."

Clay Adams paused. When he started speaking again, the bitterness had left his voice. "Anyway, I heard Grady say that when a man knows others are gunnin' for him, he'll look each way careful-like and listen for any strange sounds behind him. But even the best of them sometimes forget to look up." The deputy glanced at Buck, who seemed to be getting more lucid. "Well, Mr. Grady, tonight I didn't forget."

The swinging doors of the saloon opened. Two men stepped out cautiously and approached the lawmen as they jumped to their feet.

"I suppose you gents know Buck here, he's probably a trusted coworker." Matheson slipped into his mock friendly voice.

"We know 'im," one of the men replied nervously. Both men were making a show of keeping their hands away from their guns.

The sheriff looked down at Buck, shook his head, then continued to address the two men. "Your friend here is one of the unlucky ones. After he's patched up, he'll stand trial for trying to ambush two lawmen. And Bull Grady won't be the judge. No sir, those days are over."

The lawman's voice became serious and firm. "You gents are lucky. I want you to take Buck to the General Store where the doc is. Then get on your horses and leave town. I don't want to see you back here ever again. Understand?"

"Unnerstand," both men replied, then helped their comrade to his feet and began to half carry him toward the general store.

The sheriff and his deputy watched the slow procession for a few moments. "Those men will ride off, all right," Adams said. "They might not even get poor Buck to the doc. As soon as they're outta view they might drop him on the street and take off."

"We can tend to that later." Matheson walked into the Fighting Bull with his deputy a step behind him.

Inside, the saloon looked eerie. The place was empty of people except for the bartender and four men who sat around one round table. Two empty chairs were situated haphazardly at the table. They had, no doubt, been filled by the two men who might already be riding out of town. The bartender tried to look busy as the lawmen walked in, but the men at the table did nothing except watch the newcomers.

The sheriff smiled, turned to his deputy, and spoke loudly. "I heard that Bull Grady's been having trouble keeping help around lately; looks like he's even lost his piano player and saloon girls. No wonder he hasn't got any customers to speak of."

At a nod from his boss, Clay Adams positioned himself against a wall where he could watch the curious group of men that now populated the Fighting Bull Saloon. Boyd Matheson walked over to the bar and leaned over the counter.

"Sorry to wake you up, barkeep, but could I have a deck of cards?"

The bartender's hands shook as he placed a deck of cards in front of the lawman. One quick glance into the man's eyes was all Matheson needed to confirm that the bartender was terrified. That made him dangerous. Matheson knew that there was at least one gun somewhere under the bar and he didn't want it in the hands of a confused, frightened man.

"You know barkeep, they got laws some places about bars not being open on election day until the polls close. I think we should do that right here in Gradyville."

The bartender's voice quivered, "Election day ain't until tomorra, Sheriff."

Matheson smiled broadly. "It's past midnight. Tomorrow is here. I'm ordering you to leave, barkeep. Don't worry about Bull Grady or those jaspers at the table. Come sunup, they'll be gone or in jail."

The bartender's eyes shifted from Matheson to the men at the table and briefly shot upwards to Bull Grady's office. Then he made his move. Stumbling once, the man ran around the bar and out the swinging front doors.

Matheson turned to Clay Adams who was still standing against the wall, his eyes on the four men at the table. "No piano player, no girls and now this place doesn't even have a barkeep." The sheriff clucked his tongue. " 'I would say this is an establishment in desperate need of new ownership."

Matheson walked over to the table and dropped the deck of cards in the center. "You gents will just have to keep yourselves entertained with a friendly game of cards. I might join you later; right now, since the barkeep's gone, I guess I'll have to pour myself a drink."

The sheriff took one loud step toward the bar, then moved quickly to the set of heavy curtains that covered the window to the right of the bar. Those curtains were now slightly parted.

Matheson drew his gun, then, using his left hand, he jerked loose the rod that ran over the window and tossed the curtains to the floor. He smashed the window with his gun, reached out and grabbed the arm of a man who was stationed outside.

"Step inside, careful and slow. Keep your hands away from your gun." Matheson let go of the man's arm, but kept his Colt pointed at his adversary crawling clumsily through the window.

"Do you know this gent, deputy?" Matheson asked.

"Calls himself Bert," Adams replied.

"Bert, I think your friends are in need of another hand for poker." He pushed Bert toward the table where the deck of cards remained untouched in the center.

Bert sat down on one of the abandoned chairs.

Matheson holstered his Colt and quickly circled the table relieving each man of his gun. To Clay Adams it seemed only a few seconds before a pile of pistols was lying on the floor beside him.

"Don't think any of these gents are carrying anything extra on them. But keep a careful eye just the same," Matheson spoke quietly to his deputy.

The sheriff's voice became loud again as he nodded toward the broken window. "I can sure understand why Bull Grady wanted to keep that window covered. That window offers a perfect view of the outside stairs that lead to the back door of Grady's office."

Matheson grinned at Clay Adams. "Why, you have a wonderful view here, deputy. You can watch these gents play cards and keep an eye on the back stairs while you do."

Adams tried to match the exaggerated good humor of his boss. "If I see someone goin' up them stairs I just might fire my pistol, so you can give them a greetin' all proper-like."

"Good idea." Matheson walked over to the table and pointed to the cards. "If you jaspers don't feel like poker maybe you can play old maid. But play like gentlemen. That way, maybe you'll all get to leave town tonight."

Boyd Matheson gave his deputy a quick nod, then he slowly ascended the stairway and walked toward Bull Grady's office. Even without all the commotion Matheson and Adams had just created downstairs, Grady would be expecting a visit from the law. His gang of thugs had been decimated, but Grady was still a very dangerous man.

One knock on Bull Grady's office was all that was needed. "Come on in!" The voice rang with a bombastic cheerfulness.

As Matheson entered the room his chest tightened and he began to feel slightly dizzy. A thick haze of cigar smoke filled the room. The lawman had forgotten to take Grady's love of cigars into account. He hoped he hadn't overlooked anything else.

The lawman glanced to his left and saw an open door. He hadn't even noticed that door on his first visit to the office, probably because he was too preoccupied trying to mask his nausea from the cigar smoke.

Laughter boomed from behind the door as if mocking the lawman's carelessness. Bull Grady stepped into the room, blowing smoke and waving his cigar. " 'Well, well. Evening, Sheriff. Was that you making all that noise downstairs?"

Matheson's eyes spotted a bed and a dresser in the side room. Bull Grady caught the surprise in his visitor's glance. "Yeah, I live here. My wife died years ago. No kids. I sold the ranch back then. Now I devote my time to running my mines, my saloons, my town."

"It's not your town anymore, Grady. I'm here to arrest you."

Matheson had wanted that statement to rattle Bull Grady. It didn't work. Grady walked behind his desk and stood there, looking at the lawman with a blend of amusement and contempt. "And just what is the charge?"

Boyd Matheson had to cough before he could speak. "We'll start with attempted kidnapping. You also tried to fix an election. All sorts of laws against that. You've had so many people killed, it's a shame I can't hang you. But I can put you in jail for twenty years or more. Guess that will make me happy enough."

Grady blew a stream of smoke in the lawman's direction then laughed. "Sheriff, how did you manage to stay alive this long? Wheeler!"

Pete Wheeler stepped through the open side door into Grady's office. He held a Colt .44 aimed directly at Matheson.

Bull Grady chuckled with what seemed to be genuine amusement. "I left the door open on purpose. If I had closed the door, you would have suspected someone else was in that room."

"You're a smart man." Matheson said in a mocking voice.

Bull Grady flicked an ash from his cigar. The gesture was oddly threatening, as if he could dispose of Matheson as easily. "Let me tell you just how smart I am. We're going to kill you right now and toss your body down the back stairs. Right Pete?"

"That's right, Mr. Grady." A smirk slashed across Wheeler's face. He jerked his left thumb at the back door. "I watched you yank those curtains down. Reckon your deputy is keepin' an eye on things below. When he sees your body fallin' down the stairway, he'll come runnin' to help." Pete Wheeler lifted his gun a bit higher. " 'That's when I put a couple of slugs in him."

Bull Grady leaned forward, placing one arm on his desk. "We get the boys downstairs and clear out the jail cells, then we move on the general store. We kill everyone, including the girl."

Dizziness mixed with panic as Matheson tried to

stay resolute. He needed to find a weakness in one of the two men and exploit it. And he needed to breathe quicker and not inhale too deeply. Much more cigar smoke in his lungs and he would be on the floor in a coughing spasm.

"You don't look so good, Sheriff," Grady said.

"Maybe he's thinkin' about the girl," Wheeler cut in. "If he'd let things be, the girl woulda spent a few nights in a cave and that's all. Now she's gonna die. I want you to think about that right before I shoot you, Matheson."

Boyd Matheson coughed, cleared his throat, then spoke in a lighthearted manner. "I got other things to think about, Pete. Like how the whole town's going to be laughing at you."

"Whaddya mean?"

"Folks know you can't take me in a fair fight. Remember when I made you prance out of that general store with an empty holster? How many men did you have with you that day, Pete? There were three of you, as I remember."

Bull Grady waved his cigar nervously in Wheeler's direction. " 'Kill him! Now!"

Matheson feigned a laugh and shook his head. "Then there was that big show yesterday in front of my office. The whole dang town must have been watching. I shot those tin cans a whole lot better than you did. Then I ripped that badge right off your shirt. You whimpered away like a kicked dog. Now folks are going to hear about how you had to shoot me down without a fight. Grady will have a little too much of his own rotgut some night and spill what happened. Reckon folks will be laughing about that for years."

Wheeler twirled his gun in his hand, then dropped the weapon back into its holster. "I'm gonna shut you up right now."

Matheson fought back his dizziness and nausea. At that moment the entire room became vivid and stark as if every detail were a matter of life and death. The sheriff saw Wheeler's chest move as he breathed. He heard the desk drawer open a few inches and heard the rattle of a derringer inside. Matheson saw cigar smoke twirl in the air like a viper searching for prey. He saw Wheeler's jaw move up slightly as his hand moved down. The shot from his own gun sounded like an explosion to the lawman. He expected the building to crumble as Pete Wheeler slammed against a wall and fell to the floor. Wheeler's pistol reflected light as it skidded toward the sheriff. He turned and yelled at Bull Grady in a raspy voice. " 'Drop that gun. It's over."

The derringer made a clattering sound as it journeyed from Grady's hand to the edge of the desk to the floor. Bull Grady laughed but the look in his eyes was now one of terror.

"I'm rich Matheson, and I can make you rich." Grady's cigar dropped from his hand. He didn't seem to notice. "Join up with me. You won't regret it."

"How about Pete?" Matheson looked down at

Wheeler who was twitching in pain. "He knows everything. He may not like me taking his job."

"Kill him!" Grady spoke in a loud whisper. "You're
the sheriff. I'll back whatever story you use. Kill him!"

Pete Wheeler gazed at his boss with an expression
that went from shock to hatred. Matheson figured that
Wheeler would gladly join the Tibbs brothers and testify against his former boss. At that moment Matheson
realized that his earlier statement was true.

It was all over.

Chapter Sixteen

The sight of Boyd Matheson escorting Bull Grady and a staggering Pete Wheeler out of the Fighting Bull Saloon and into jail was all it took to rid Gradyville of the remains of Bull Grady's gang. By sunrise, the only living gang members still in town were the ones in jail or the ones moved to Doc Evans' home to recuperate from their wounds.

With the town's founder in jail, the election for mayor became an almost festive occasion. Citizens hung around Remick's General Store, joking and congratulating Reverend Stubby on his victory long before the ballots were counted.

The actual results ridded Gradyville of one more undesirable resident. After receiving only a handful of votes, Clarence Potts, the incumbent mayor and Bull

Grady's puppet, hastily sold his hardware store and left town.

"It ain't right," Deputy Clay Adams grumbled upon hearing of Clarence's departure. "Potts was in cahoots with Bull Grady. He ought to be in jail."

"Yeah, he ought to be," Boyd Matheson agreed. "But in a small frontier town things don't always go the way they oughtta. You have to settle for what you can do. And we've done plenty."

The trial of Bull Grady and his henchmen had to wait several weeks until a circuit judge could make it to Gradyville. This time around Gradyville's new mayor, Reverend Stubby, represented the prosecution while Jeb Crane served as defense attorney.

Pete Wheeler's hatred for his former boss became apparent soon after the trial began. Wheeler testified that Grady had ordered him and another gang member to kill Sheriff George Stuart from the alley beside the sheriff's office and frame Boyd Matheson for the murder. The other gang member involved in the murder had been killed during the attack on the church.

After Wheeler's testimony, the Tibbs brothers further stoked the fire with their tale of being hired by Grady to kidnap Laurel Remick. The Tibbs' were followed by confessions from Grady's less prominent gunslingers, all of them hoping for reduced sentences in exchange for their cooperation.

Reverend Stubby specifically asked the jury not to hang any of the defendants. "I'm not saying that hanging is wrong," the pastor stated in his summation. "But the west will never become the place we want it to be until folks realize that taking a human life is a very serious matter. For his cooperation and testimony Pete Wheeler deserves to live. And I would ask you to consider all of Bull Grady's life before you sentence him to the rope."

Both Bull Grady and Pete Wheeler were sentenced to life in prison. Lesser sentences were handed out to the Tibbs brothers and the smaller fish in Grady's gang.

The defendants were taken to a territorial prison at the end of the trial. The only exception was Bull Grady. Grady became ill during the trial and had to recuperate in the town's jail.

"He has a bad case of pneumonia," Doc Evans told Boyd Matheson while the two were alone in the sheriff's office. "It will take several weeks before he can be moved."

"I've listened to that cough of his," Matheson spoke softly. "Grady smoked a lot of stogies. Could he have the same thing as me?"

Doc Evans nodded his head and left the office.

The Bull Grady that a federal marshal escorted out of jail to be taken to the territorial prison was a much different man than the tyrant who had ruled the town for years. Grady had lost a lot of weight, and excess skin hung on him like melted candle wax.

"Could you stay with the prisoner for a moment, Sheriff? I need to talk to the driver."

Matheson nodded assent to the marshal, who stepped off the boardwalk and began talking with the federal deputy who would be driving the coach. The sheriff couldn't help but smile to himself. It all looked a bit silly. One coach and two federal lawmen to drive a frail old man to prison. But maybe they were thinking about the Bull Grady that once was.

The old man who now stood on the boardwalk in front of the sheriff's office looked about the town with a stunned wonderment. No one was looking at him. The town of Gradyville was going on as normal, indifferent to the fact that its founder was leaving forever.

"Hello, Bull."

Bull Grady seemed startled as his head turned toward the speaker. Like the sheriff, standing on his other side, Grady had not heard Reverend Stubby approaching.

"I thought you might appreciate this." The pastor held out a Bible. Grady looked the other way and didn't accept it.

"I know you haven't said anything for several weeks, Bull, and maybe that's for the best," Reverend Stubby said. "But I know you've been listening."

The pastor smiled and continued. "Gradyville is small, and news gets around quick. You've heard that the town council wants to change the name of this town. Well, I'm going to oppose it. This place wouldn't be here if it wasn't for you. I'm not going to let folks forget that. The good things you did should be remembered as well as the bad."

Bull Grady remained silent but his face contorted. He turned around to Reverend Stubby and nodded his head as he accepted the Bible.

"We're ready, Sheriff Matheson." The federal marshal escorted Bull Grady into the coach and sat across from him. As the coach pulled away, Bull Grady waved weakly to the two men on the boardwalk.

"He'll be dead within a year." Matheson suddenly stopped speaking. He realized that those words could also apply to him, and quickly changed the subject. "I guess it's a good thing you're doing, Reverend, persuading the council to keep the name of the town. But that's a lot of trouble to be saving the soul of a killer."

"Saving Bull Grady's soul is only a part of it, Sheriff. I'm thinking about all the souls in this town."

"I don't follow you, Reverend."

The pastor slowly looked about, his eyes scanning the entire street. "Bull Grady was a builder, and in his younger days he helped other people build. But Grady forgot that all things come from the Lord. Grady began to think of himself as the source of all power. Before long, he began to expect other people to worship him."

Reverend Stubby turned to the sheriff with a stark gaze. "This town's name is both an inspiration and a warning. Our town is named after a man who started off well, but allowed pride to destroy him and turn him into a vicious killer. Yes, Gradyville is a fine name for this place."

A slight smile softened the pastor's gaze. "That's enough sermon for now. I'll see you tomorrow morning, Sheriff."

Reverend Stubby walked off, leaving Matheson a bit confused about the "tomorrow morning" remark. After a few moments, the lawman broke into a soft chuckle.

"Of course," Matheson whispered to himself. "Tomorrow is Sunday."

Two weeks after Bull Grady left for territorial prison, Boyd Matheson came in early to the office to catch up on paperwork. Clay Adams had closed up the office the previous night, so it was close to nine before the deputy arrived.

Adams nodded to his boss. "Already had my coffee; I'll get started on the round—"

"I've already done it."

"Wha—"

"You and I are tracking Orin Mellor this morning."

"We don't have to track him. Orin's over at the livery with his pa."

"No. He left town an hour ago. I asked him to. I want you to get some experience tracking"

"I can do that just fine."

"I know you can hunt animals. But how about tracking a man who knows you're on his trail? A man who is trying to fool you? Ever done much of that?"

Clay Adams sighed and shook his head. "Guess not. I'll wait outside." A shot of bright light came into the office as the deputy walked out.

Matheson put his paperwork away and reflected on how well Clay Adams was coming along in his job. Just then a familiar bark interrupted his musings.

The sheriff got up and moved stealthily to the small office window. He peered outside and saw his deputy with Laurel Remick. The couple had their backs to the window. Clay Adams was crouched over Perkins, carefully petting the dog. "He sure is frisky. Can't tell he's ever been hurt."

"The doctor took his bandages off last week," Laurel said.

Perkins seemed to like Clay Adams. Good thing, Matheson thought. The sheriff moved away from the window and busied himself in the office. He waited until Perkins' bark began to recede in the distance before putting on his hat.

As he opened the door of the office, the sheriff saw Clay Adams sitting on his horse with his eyes focused on Laurel Remick, who was walking toward the general store. The look on Adams' face was completely ridiculous and Matheson figured he must have looked the same way that first day he met Ann.

The deputy's eyes suddenly snapped back to his boss. "What are you laughin' at?"

The sheriff shook his head. "That would take too

long to explain and you wouldn't much appreciate the answer."

Boyd Matheson laughed once more, closed the door behind him and stepped into the sunshine.